He Was Going To Kiss Her.

Releasing her wrist, he put one finger beneath her chin and lifted her face to his. "Relax and let me..."

He couldn't wait any longer and dropped his head to fasten his mouth on hers, kissing her hard and deep, pouring all the longing and frustration of the past two years into the embrace. He felt her hands clench on his shoulders, but she wasn't pushing him away. Oh, no. He felt the way she melted against him, the way her fingers dug into his flesh and he knew she was going to be his again.

But this time, Wade promised himself, he wouldn't leave her without a word.

Dear Reader,

This April, leave the showers behind and embrace the warmth found only in a Silhouette Desire novel. First off is Susan Crosby's *The Forbidden Twin*, the latest installment in the scintillating continuity THE ELLIOTTS. This time, bad girl twin Scarlet sets her heart on seducing the one man she can't have. And speaking of wanting what you can't have, Peggy Moreland's *The Texan's Forbidden Affair* begins a brand-new series for this *USA TODAY* bestselling author. A PIECE OF TEXAS introduces a fabulous Lone Star legacy and stories that will stay with you long after the book is done.

Also launching this month is Maureen Child's SUMMER OF SECRETS, a trilogy about three handsome-as-sin cousins who are in for a season of scandalous revelations...and it all starts with *Expecting Lonergan's Baby*. Katherine Garbera wraps up her WHAT HAPPENS IN VEGAS...series with *Their Million-Dollar Night*. What woman could resist a millionaire who doesn't care about her past as long as she's willing to share his bed?

Making her Silhouette Desire debut this month is Silhouette Intimate Moments and HQN Books author Catherine Mann, with *Baby, I'm Yours*. Her delectable hero is certainly one guy this heroine should think about saying "I do" to once that pregnancy test comes back positive. And rounding out the month with a story of long-denied passion and shocking secrets is Anne Marie Winston's *The Soldier's Seduction*.

Enjoy all we have to offer this month!

Melissa Jeglinski

Melissa Jeglinski
Senior Editor
Silhouette Desire

Please address questions and book requests to:
Silhouette Reader Service
U.S.: 3010 Walden Ave., P.O. Box 1325, Buffalo, NY 14269
Canadian: P.O. Box 609, Fort Erie, Ont. L2A 5X3

ANNE MARIE WINSTON

The Soldier's Seduction

Published by Silhouette Books
America's Publisher of Contemporary Romance

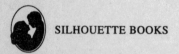

SILHOUETTE BOOKS

ISBN 0-373-76722-6

THE SOLDIER'S SEDUCTION

Copyright © 2006 by Anne Marie Rodgers

This edition published by arrangement with Harlequin Books S.A.

® and TM are trademarks of Harlequin Books S.A., used under license.
Trademarks indicated with ® are registered in the United States Patent
and Trademark Office, the Canadian Trade Marks Office and in other
countries.

Visit Silhouette Books at www.eHarlequin.com

Printed in U.S.A.

Books by Anne Marie Winston

Silhouette Desire

Best Kept Secrets #742
Island Baby #770
Chance at a Lifetime #809
Unlikely Eden #827
Carolina on My Mind #845
Substitute Wife #863
Find Her, Keep Her #887
Rancher's Wife #936
Rancher's Baby #1031
Seducing the Proper Miss Miller #1155
*The Baby Consultant #1191
*Dedicated to Deirdre #1197
*The Bride Means Business #1204
Lovers' Reunion #1226
The Pregnant Princess #1268
Seduction, Cowboy Style #1287
Rancher's Proposition #1322
Tall, Dark & Western #1339
A Most Desirable M.D. #1371
Risqué Business #1407
Billionaire Bachelors: Ryan #1413
Billionaire Bachelors: Stone #1423
Billionaire Bachelors: Garrett #1440
Billionaire Bachelors: Gray #1526
Born To Be Wild #1538
The Marriage Ultimatum #1562
The Enemy's Daughter #1603
For Services Rendered #1617
The Soldier's Seduction #1722

Silhouette Books

Broken Silence
"Invitation to Seduction"

Family Secrets
Pyramid of Lies

Logan's Legacy
The Homecoming

*Butler County Brides

ANNE MARIE WINSTON

RITA® Award finalist and bestselling author Anne Marie Winston loves babies she can give back when they cry, animals in all shapes and sizes and just about anything that blooms. When she's not writing, she's managing a house full of animals and teenagers, reading anything she can find and trying *not* to eat chocolate. She will dance at the slightest provocation and weeds her garden when she can't see the sun for the weeds anymore. You can learn more about Anne Marie's novels by visiting her Web site at www.annemariewinston.com.

Dedicated to the memory of those animals who perished when they were left behind during Hurricane Katrina and with warmest thanks to every rescuer and animal lover who responded and saved so many others

One

It wasn't what he'd expected.

Wade brought the rental car to a halt along the curb and simply absorbed the sight of the modest, cozy home nestled in the small-town neighborhood. Phoebe's home. Phoebe's neighborhood.

He cut the ignition and eased himself from the car, taking in the pretty autumn wreath on the front door, the carved pumpkin on the second of the brick steps leading to the porch, the fall flowers in bright shades of rust, burgundy and gold that brightened up the bare spaces in front of the small bushes along the foundation.

He'd assumed she would live in an apartment. He didn't really know why he'd thought that, but every time he'd pictured Phoebe since he'd learned she had moved away, he'd imagined her living in an apartment or a small condo. Nothing so…permanent, as this house appeared to be.

He'd gotten quite a shock when he'd finally returned home, eagerly anticipating his first sight of her—only to learn that she'd left California months earlier. He didn't even want to think about the bleak misery that had swept through him, the letdown that had been so overwhelming that he'd just wanted to sit down and cry.

Not that he ever would. Soldiers didn't cry. Especially soldiers who had been decorated all to hell and back.

Living at home had been difficult. Only two short months before he'd been injured, he'd gone home on leave for his mother's funeral. While he was recuperating, his father made valiant attempts to keep things as normal around the house as possible. But without his mother, there was a big hole nothing could disguise.

He made casual inquiries about where Phoebe had gone, but no one seemed to know. By the time he was home for a month, he was desperate enough to start digging. The secretary of her high school graduating class had no forwarding address. A light Internet search turned up nothing. He finally thought to call Berkeley, the university she'd attended, but they wouldn't, or couldn't, give him any information.

He was about ready to consider hiring a private investigator when he thought of calling June, the only girl other than Phoebe's twin sister Melanie who he could really remember Phoebe hanging around with in high school. Geeky little June with her thick glasses and straight *A*s. Someone Melanie wouldn't have been caught dead hanging out with, but as he recalled, a genuinely sweet kid.

They really had seemed like kids to his four-years-older eyes back then. But by the time the twins had graduated from high school, those years had no longer seemed to be of much consequence.

Getting in touch with Phoebe's old friend was a stroke of luck. June had gotten a Christmas card from Phoebe four months after she'd moved. And God bless her, she'd kept the address.

That address had been quite a shock. She'd gone from California clear across the country to a small town in rural New York state.

Ironically, it was a familiar area. Phoebe's new home was less than an hour from West Point, where he'd spent four long years in a gray uniform chafing for graduation day, when he could finally become a real soldier.

He wouldn't have been so impatient for those days to end if he'd known what lay ahead of him.

He climbed the small set of steps carefully. His doctors were sure he'd make a full recovery—full enough for civilian life, anyway. But the long flight from San Diego to JFK had been more taxing than he'd anticipated. He probably should have gotten a room for the night, looked up Phoebe tomorrow when he was rested.

But he hadn't been able to make himself wait a moment longer.

He knocked on the wooden front door, eyeing the wavy glass diamond pane in the door's upper portion. Although it was designed to obscure a good view of the home's occupants, he might be able to see someone coming toward the door. But after a few moments and two more knocks, nobody showed. Phoebe wasn't home.

Disappointment swamped him. He leaned his head against the door frame, completely spent. He'd counted on seeing her so badly. But…he glanced at his watch. He hadn't even considered the time. It was barely four o'clock.

The last time he'd seen her, she was a year out of college with a degree in elementary education, and she'd been teaching first grade. If she still was a teacher, she might soon be getting home. She probably worked, he decided as relief seeped through him.

If she wasn't married, he thought, trying to encourage himself, it stood to reason she'd need income. And June hadn't heard anything about a husband. If she had married, she hadn't taken his name, which didn't really fit with the quiet, traditional girl he'd known so well. And he knew she hadn't taken anyone's name because he'd checked the local phone book and found her there: P. Merriman.

Fine. He'd wait. He turned and started for his car, but a porch swing piled with pillows caught his attention. He'd just sit there and wait for her.

If she'd been married, he wouldn't be here, he assured himself. If she'd been married, he would have left her alone, wouldn't have attempted to contact her again in this lifetime.

But he was pretty sure she wasn't.

And despite the good reasons he had for staying away from Phoebe Merriman, despite the fact that he'd behaved like a jerk the last time they'd been together, he'd never been able to forget her. Never been able to convince himself that being with her had been a mistake. He'd thought of little else during his long months of recuperation and therapy. He'd nearly reached out to her then, but some part of him had shied away from a phone call or an e-mail.

He wanted to see her in person when he asked her if there was any chance she'd let him into her life again. Sighing, he dragged one of the pillows up and leaned his head against it. If only things hadn't gotten so screwed up at the end.

It had been bad enough that Phoebe's twin Melanie had died because of him. Indirectly, maybe, but it still had been his fault.

He'd compounded it in the biggest damn way possible when he'd made love to Phoebe after the funeral. And then he'd run.

Phoebe Merriman jumped when the mobile phone in her minivan began to play the jazzy tune she'd programmed into it. That phone hardly ever rang. The only reason she had it, really, was so that Bridget's babysitter could always reach her in case of an emergency.

Alarmed, she punched the button to take the call. A quick glance at the display had the dread in her stomach lurching uncomfortably. Phoebe had good reason to fear unexpected phone calls. And just as she'd feared, it was her home number. "Hello?"

"Phoebe?" The babysitter, Angie, sounded breathless.

"Angie. What's wrong?"

"There's a man sitting on the front porch. In the swing."

The news was almost anticlimactic, considering that she'd been fearing a high fever, blood or broken bones.

"Sitting? And what else?"

"Nothing else." Phoebe realized Angie wasn't breathless; she was whispering. "He came to the door but I didn't answer, so he sat down on the swing and I thought I'd better call you." Her voice quavered a little.

Phoebe remembered how young her sitter was, newly graduated from high school and still living with her parents on the next street over, taking evening classes at a local community college. Phoebe had met Angie's mother in her Sunday-school class and had felt lucky to find Angie.

"You did exactly right," she assured the younger woman. "If all he's doing is sitting there, just stay inside with the doors closed. I'm only a few blocks from home."

She pulled into her driveway a few minutes later, the cell phone's line still open. There was a gray sedan with a rental tag parked in front of her house. Maybe it belonged to whoever was waiting on her front porch.

"Okay, Angie," she said. "I'm home. You stay right where you are until I come inside."

She took a deep breath. Should she call the police? Common sense told her whoever was waiting on her porch probably wasn't a criminal. Otherwise, he wouldn't be here in the middle of the day, unconcerned about the neighbors taking down his license plate or identifying him. She positioned her keys between her fingers with one key thrust outward, as she'd learned in the self-defense class she'd taken when she'd first started college. Then she pivoted on her heel and headed up her front walk.

She started up the porch steps, unable to see the swing because of the trellis of roses blooming across the front of the porch. She knew from experience that a person sitting there on the swing could see out much more easily than anyone could see in.

As she reached the porch, a very large man came into view. Adrenaline rushed through her as he began to rise from the swing. She angled her body to confront him.

"What are—*Wade!*"

As the man's identity registered, a wave of shock slammed into her. It couldn't be.

Wade was dead.

Her knees felt as if they might buckle and she groped for the railing behind her. The keys fell to the floor with a loud jangle. "You—you're Wade." An inane statement. Of course it was Wade.

He was smiling but his eyes were watchful as he took a step forward. "Yeah. Hi, Phoebe."

"B-b-but…"

His smile faded as she took a step backward. One eyebrow rose in a quirk as familiar to her as her own smile in the mirror. That quizzical expression had been only one of the things she'd loved about Wade Donnelly. "But what?" he asked quietly.

"I thought you were dead!" She blurted out the words as her legs gave way and she sank to the top step, dropping her head onto her knees as incredulity warred with a strong desire to cry hysterically.

Footsteps rang out as Wade crossed the porch and then the boards of the top step depressed as he sat down beside her. One large hand touched her back. "My God," she said, the words muffled. "You really are here, aren't you?"

"I'm really here." It was definitely Wade, his distinctly masculine tone one she would recognize anywhere. He touched her back again, just one small uncertain touch, and she had to fight the urge to throw herself into his arms.

He never really belonged to me, she reminded herself.

"I'm sorry it's such a shock." His voice was quiet and deep and rang with sincerity. "I *was* presumed to be dead for a couple of days until I could get back to my unit. But that was months ago."

"How long have you been home?" He'd been deployed right after Melanie's funeral. The memory brought back others she'd tried to forget, as well, and she focused on his answer, trying to ignore the past.

"About five weeks. I've been trying to find you." He hesitated for a moment. "June gave me your address and she knew I survived. I assumed she— or someone back home—had told you."

"No." She shook her head without lifting it. She'd stopped reading the news from home the day she'd read his obituary. And though she'd sent June a Christmas card this year, they hadn't exchanged more than signatures since she'd moved.

Silence fell. She sensed that he didn't know what to say any more than she did—

Bridget! Shocked that she could have forgotten her own child for a moment—particularly this moment—Phoebe leaped to her feet, ignoring Wade's startled exclamation. "Just—ah, just let me put my things inside," she said. "Then we can talk."

Her hands trembled as she turned away from the man she'd loved throughout her adolescent years and into young womanhood. The keys were slippery in her sweaty grasp and she dropped them again. Before she could react, Wade came to her side and stretched down for the keys.

"Here."

"Thank you." She took the keys carefully, without touching his hand, fumbled the correct one into the lock and opened her front door.

Reality hit her in the face again. Wade Donnelly was alive and waiting to talk to her. And she had to tell him she'd borne his child.

Angie rushed forward as Phoebe came through the door and closed it firmly behind herself. Before the sitter could speak, Phoebe put her finger to her lips to indicate silence. She walked through the front rooms toward the back of the little house and dropped her things onto the kitchen table. "Listen," she said to Angie in a quiet tone, "there's nothing to worry about. He's an old friend I haven't seen in a long time. Can you stay a little longer in case Bridget wakes up?"

Angie nodded, her eyes wide. "Sure."

"We're going to talk outside. "I don't—I'm not inviting him in and I don't particularly want him to know about Bridget, so please don't come out."

Angie nodded, an uncharacteristically knowing smile crossing her face. "No problem. I wouldn't want to cause trouble for you."

Phoebe paused in the act of walking back through the living room. "Cause trouble for me?"

"With people back where you came from." Angie gestured vaguely. "I mean, I know everybody has babies without getting married these days, but if you don't want anyone back home to know, that's your business."

Phoebe felt her eyebrows rising practically to her hairline. She opened her mouth, then closed it abruptly before hysterical laughter could bubble out. Dear innocent Angie thought she was hiding Bridget because she was ashamed of having an illegitimate child. If only it were that simple!

She swallowed as she slipped through the front door again, closing it securely behind her. Wade was standing now, leaning against one of the porch posts, dwarfing the small space. Lord, she'd forgotten how big he really was.

She drank in his appearance, trying to reconcile the grief she'd carried for the past six months with the reality of seeing him alive and apparently well. His dark, wavy hair was conservatively short compared to the out-of-control locks he'd sported in high school, but quite a bit longer than the last time she'd seen him, when he'd had a high and tight military cut that had stripped every bit of curl away. If he weighed an ounce more than he had then, it wasn't noticeable; his shoulders were still wide and heavily muscled, his hips narrow and his belly flat, his legs still as powerful looking as they'd been when he'd been a running back for the high school football team. That had been almost a dozen years ago, and she'd been a silly middle-school teen at the time, already pathetically infatuated with her older, totally hot neighbor.

Then she realized he was watching her stare at him, his gray eyes as clear and piercing as always beneath the black slashes of his eyebrows. She felt her cheeks heat and she crossed her arms over her chest.

Taking a deep breath, she voiced the question burning in her mind. "Why were you reported dead if they weren't sure?" Her voice shook with the remembered agony of learning that Wade was gone forever. "I read about your funeral..." The sentence died unfinished as she realized she'd read about the *plans* for his funeral. In his obituary.

Wade blinked, but before his gaze slid away from hers, she caught a glimpse of a haunting pain. "Battlefield mistake," he said. "They found my dog tags but not my body. By the time the mistake was corrected, word had already gone out that I'd been KIA."

She put a hand to her mouth, fighting the tears that desperately wanted to escape. All these months she'd thought he was dead….

"I was injured," he said. "In the chaos that followed the explosion, a friendly Afghani hid me. It took the guy three days to make contact with American troops, and it wasn't until then that the mistake was caught. The fellow who died whom they'd assumed was me had already been shipped to Germany for autopsy. They'd have caught the mistake eventually, but I sure gave a lot of people a shock. And just for the record," he added, "Mom and Dad didn't actually have a funeral. It was planned, then canceled. I guess you didn't attend or you'd have found out."

She opened her mouth, then closed it again and simply shook her head. She still wanted to cry. Badly. *I was having your baby at the time* was so not the thing to say.

She risked a glance at him and was almost undone by the pain in his eyes.

Unable to bear being the cause of that pain, she said, "I couldn't come back for the funeral." She turned away and settled on the porch swing. "It took every penny I had to move here." *Well, that wasn't a lie.* She'd been lucky to find this place, luckier still that, although she had few assets, her credit history was good and with the teachers' credit union behind her, she'd been able to qualify for a mortgage. It hadn't hurt that the cost of living in California was so much higher than it was here. She'd never have been able to afford even this modest little home if she'd stayed on the West Coast.

"Why did you move?" he asked suddenly. "All the way across the country? I know you don't have any family to keep you in California, but that's where you grew up, where your roots are. Don't you miss it?"

She swallowed. "Of course I miss it." *Terribly. I miss the cobblestones on the beaches and the freezing cold water, the balmy days and cooler nights that rarely vary. I miss driving down to Point Loma, or over to Cardiff, and watching whale migrations in the fall. I even miss the insanity of driving on the freeway and the fire danger. Most of all, I miss you.* "But my life is here now."

"Why?"

She raised her eyebrows. "Why what?"

"What makes rural New York state so special that you have to live here?"

She shrugged. "I'm a teacher. I'll have tenure in two more years and I don't want to start over again somewhere else. The pay is good here and the cost of living is more manageable than in Southern California."

He nodded. "I see." He joined her on the swing, sitting close but not touching. He placed an arm along the back of the swing and turned slightly toward her. "It's good to see you." His voice was warm, his eyes even more so.

She could barely breathe. He was looking at her the way she'd dreamed of for years. Years when he'd been too old for her to do more than dream of, years when he'd been her sister's boyfriend, more recently when she'd thought he was dead and she was raising his child alone.

"Wade..." She reached out a hand and placed her palm gently against his cheek. "I'm so glad you're alive. It's good to see you, too, but—"

"Have dinner with me tonight."

"I can't." Fear infused her voice with a touch of panic. She started to withdraw her hand but he covered it with his, turning his face into her palm, and she felt the warmth of his lips whispering against the tender skin.

"Tomorrow night, then."

"I—"

"Phoeber, I'm not taking no for an answer." The silly childhood nickname gave the moment an even deeper intimacy. "I'm not leaving here until you say yes."

She stepped back a full pace as he finally released her hand. Dinner was a bad idea, given the way her heart still pounded at the mere sight of him.

She'd grown up in the months since she'd become a parent. She no longer believed in the kind of love she read about in romance novels. At least, not mutual love that was returned. And she'd stopped allowing herself to believe that what had happened between Wade and her that day at the cabin had been anything but his reaction to the shock of her sister's death.

Now Wade was here, back from the dead, untying every neatly packed-away detail in her memories. Confusing her, rousing feelings she hadn't let herself feel in more than a year, the warmth of possibilities in his eyes scaring her to death.

She wanted to go back an hour, to come home as always to an empty porch and no tough conversations.

But she had to tell him about Bridget.

It was the last thing she wanted to do, but she had to. A few weeks before she thought he had died, she'd realized she couldn't keep Wade's child from him. Telling him in an e-mail or on the phone was unthinkable, however. She'd been planning to visit him, wherever he was stationed, as soon as she could travel again, and a promise was a promise. Even if it was only to herself.

But not yet. She could hardly just invite him in, not with the bassinet and high chair, the board books and infant toys, unmistakable signs of a baby in residence. And anyway, Angie had class tonight so she wouldn't be able to stay much longer. Phoebe needed to get rid of him, plan the best way to tell him of his fatherhood.

"All right," she finally said. "Dinner tomorrow night because I have something to tell you." The words nearly choked her.

Wade raised an eyebrow in question, but when she didn't elaborate he made no comment. All he said was "Shall I pick you up at seven?"

"I'll meet you," she said quickly. "Are you staying in town?"

As it turned out, he was staying at a hotel on the other side of town. Attached to it was a restaurant that she knew had somewhat secluded booths along the walls, so she suggested they meet there. Then she stood on the porch and watched as he walked to the gray sedan.

He smiled at her over the roof of the car before he climbed in. "See you tomorrow night."

She nodded, her heart stuttering at the warmth

in his eyes, even though she reminded herself it wasn't anything more than friendship she saw there. "See you then."

But as she watched him drive away, she wondered if it wouldn't just be easier to vanish, the way people in the witness protection program did. Anything had to be easier than telling Wade he was the father of a child. Her child.

Memories bombarded her....

She was twelve. Her twin sister Melanie perched beside her on a pink bike exactly like Phoebe's purple one, and they both watched the neighborhood boys playing baseball on the local park's grassy ball field.

"I'm gonna marry Wade when I grow up,"
Melanie announced.

Phoebe frowned. "He's going to be grown up before we are. What if he marries somebody else?"
The thought of Wade Donnelly marrying anybody made her feel all twisted up inside. Wade lived across the street from them, and he was four years older than they were. Phoebe had had a crush on him since before she could remember.

"He won't marry anybody else," Melanie said confidently. "I'm going to make him love me."

And she had.

When they were seniors in high school,

Melanie had initiated her move. Phoebe went to the prom with Tim DeGrange, a friend from her Latin class. Melanie had asked Wade, even though he had just graduated from West Point that year, and to Phoebe's shock he had said yes. Prom night had been long and miserable. Melanie had clung to Wade all evening. He'd looked so handsome in his brand-new dress uniform that he'd made Phoebe's heart hurt, and she'd been suddenly so shy she could barely force herself to talk to him.

That had been the beginning. Melanie and Wade had dated through the early summer until his leave had ended and he'd headed off for his first assignment at a training school. It had been hell for Phoebe, seeing them together. But it had grown much, much worse when Melanie had begun seeing other guys while Wade was away....

"*We're not exclusive, Phoebe.*" *Melanie's voice was sharp as she responded to the censure in her twin's eyes.*

"*Wade thinks you are.*" *Phoebe was certain of that. She'd been all too aware of Wade's devotion to her sister throughout the early weeks of the summer.*

"*I'm sure he doesn't expect me to just sit at home while he's gone,*" *Melanie said.* "*It's not like he's on a short vacation. He's in the army.*"

"If you're going to date other people, you should tell him."

But Melanie hadn't listened. Which was nothing new. Melanie had never listened to Phoebe's words of warning since they'd been very small girls.

It hadn't taken Wade long to realize that Melanie's affections for him were…something less than he clearly wanted. And it had wrung Phoebe's heart when he'd come home on leave to find that Melanie wasn't waiting for him. The two had had fight after fight. They'd finally broken up for good a year and a half later, after Christmas of the girls' sophomore year in college. Phoebe only knew the details from a distance, since she'd gone to school at Berkeley, hours north of their home in Carlsbad, California. Melanie had stayed closer to home and, although the sisters had stayed in touch largely through e-mail and instant messaging, Melanie hadn't volunteered much about Wade. Phoebe, always terrified her attraction to him would be noticed, had never asked.

After Wade and Melanie had broken up, Phoebe had noticed Wade came home less and less often over the next few years. His parents, who lived two doors down the street, had occasionally mentioned his travels to her mother, but they never shared enough information to satisfy Phoebe's hungry heart. And after her mother had passed away at the end of her junior year at Berkeley, she'd heard even less.

Then came her high-school class's five-year reunion. Melanie had invited Wade…and everything had changed forever.

Two

The following evening, Wade was ready a full fifteen minutes early. He went down to the bar in the restaurant and took a seat facing the door. And barely ten minutes later, Phoebe arrived. Also early.

He took the fact that she was early as a good sign. Did she still want to be with him the way he wanted her? Yesterday's conversation on her porch had been confusing. One moment he'd have sworn she was about to fall into his arms; the next, she seemed as distant as the moon, and only slightly more talkative.

How had he missed seeing how beautiful

Phoebe was all those years they'd been living on the same damned street?

Wade knew the answer as he watched her come across the room toward him.

Both Merriman sisters had been pretty, but Melanie's dramatic coloring had always drawn more attention. Melanie had been a strawberry redhead with fair, porcelain skin, and eyes so blue they looked like a piece of the sky. Phoebe's darker, coppery curls and deeper blue eyes were equally lovely but her quiet, reserved personality kept her from joining her exuberant, vivacious sister in the limelight. Which wasn't a bad thing, he decided. Melanie had been volatile, her moods extreme, her desire for attention exhausting sometimes. Hell, most of the time, if he were honest.

She had had a sunny, sweet side and, when she was in a good mood, she was irresistible. But she'd always been excited about something, always looking for something to do.

Phoebe was calm and restful. And capable. She had always seemed very self-sufficient to him. If Melanie had had a problem, Phoebe had been the one to whom she'd turned.

Melanie. He'd successfully avoided thinking about her for a very long time. It seemed inconceivable that she wasn't leading some man in a merry dance somewhere in Southern California. Instead, she was locked forever in his memory at the age of twenty-three.

The same age Phoebe had been when he'd realized he had been chasing the wrong twin for several years.

As she drew near, he drank in every detail of her appearance. Her hair was longer than it had once been, and she wore it up in a practical twist. She had on a khaki-colored pencil-slim skirt with a sweater set in some shade of a pretty green-blue that he didn't even have a name for. Although she probably thought it was a modest outfit, the skirt ended just above her knees, showing off her slender, shapely calves and ankles, and the sleeveless top beneath the outer sweater clung enticingly to her curves. Tendrils of curls had escaped from the twist and danced around her face in the light breeze.

She was looking down at the floor rather than at him and he had a sudden moment of doubt. She'd been all he'd thought about since the last day he'd seen her. Even when he'd been in combat, or leading troops, he'd carried the memory of her deep in the recesses of his mind, where everything he couldn't afford to think about in the heat of battle lived.

Guilt—and being deployed halfway around the world—had kept him away from her in those months after the funeral, but nearly losing his life in the mountains of Afghanistan had made him realize how sorry he would be if he walked away from the possibility of a life with Phoebe.

Had he waited too long? It had been fifteen months since the fateful class reunion that had changed their lives forever, since Melanie's death and their unexpected intimacy after the funeral.

Did Phoebe regret that? Or even worse, did she blame him for Melanie's death? That niggling little fear had lodged in his brain months ago and, despite the memories of Phoebe's shining eyes at the reunion and the sweet way she'd kissed him a few days later, he couldn't shake his worry. It didn't help that deep down, he knew he *was* to blame. He'd been Melanie's date that night, he'd known how possessive she could be and yet, when he'd taken Phoebe in his arms on that dance floor, he'd forgotten everything but the wonder of what had suddenly flared between them.

After her initial shock had faded yesterday, she'd been a little too distant for comfort. She'd always been reserved, but never with him. He'd enjoyed drawing her out and making her laugh, even when they'd been young, but he'd never realized just how much he took it for granted that she relaxed around him.

On her porch last afternoon, she hadn't been relaxed.

Maybe she had a serious relationship, even though she wasn't married or engaged. He knew because one of the first things he'd done was check out her ring finger. And besides, her name hadn't changed. She had been listed as Merriman in that phone book. *I have something to tell you,* she'd said. It had sounded ominous and he'd had to struggle not to react. He sure as hell hoped she wasn't going to try to brush him off for some other guy. He'd been a clueless idiot when they were younger, had failed to realize what a treasure she was. But he knew now, and any man who thought he had a claim to Phoebe could think again.

She was going to be his.

"Hello," she said. "Is my lipstick smeared or something?"

He jolted and smiled wryly. She'd caught him staring. "No," he said honestly. "I just couldn't take my eyes off you."

Phoebe blushed as he rose and came around the table to seat her. To his astonishment, her entire pretty face turned pink.

Returning to his seat, he said, "You look beautiful. That sweater makes your eyes even bluer."

Her face was still chair. "You don't have to say

that," she said. "Melanie was the beautiful one in our family."

"One of the beautiful ones," he corrected, studying her expressionless face. "Melanie drew attention to herself and people noticed her. You did the exact opposite and managed to make yourself practically invisible most of the time. Quite a feat for a woman as beautiful as you are."

Her gaze flew to his. Finally. "Thank you," she whispered. And when their eyes met, he felt again that sudden shiver of knowledge, a "we are meant to be" moment unlike anything he'd ever felt with any other woman. He'd felt it yesterday when she'd first noticed him; if he hadn't, he wouldn't have been here now.

He could remember the first time he'd experienced it as clearly as if it *had* been yesterday. Funny that he and Phoebe had grown up in the same neighborhood, had known each other all their lives, but suddenly one night, everything had clicked into place, and he'd recognized the woman he wanted to spend forever with….

He stood by the bar and finished his soda, watching his date. Melanie sat at a table across the room on some guy's lap. She was shrieking with laughter and as Wade watched, she tilted a glass to her lips and drank. She listed to one side and nearly fell off the man's lap, and Wade suddenly realized how drunk she was. Why had he ever thought she was what he wanted?

Because you were listening to the brain in your pants, dope.

He'd been stupid to say yes when Melanie had asked him to accompany her to her first class reunion. He knew her well by then, well enough to know that Melanie didn't really want him so much as she wanted the effect she had on people when she walked in with a man in uniform. It didn't bother him anymore the way it once had, but he wasn't going to stick around here and wait for her for the rest of the evening. Phoebe had driven Melanie to meet him here, so he wasn't obligated to get her home.

He raised his glass and finished the drink, then straightened and headed for the exit.

"Wade! Wait!"

He turned at the sound of the husky female voice, his irritation fading. "Hey, Phoeber," he said. "I'm heading out. Melanie's going to catch a ride with someone else."

"You're leaving?" Her dismay was plain.

He nodded. Over the beat of the music, he said, "Yeah. I'll see you before I leave again. Promise."

"But…" Phoebe's eyes were fastened to his and he thought for a moment that she was fighting tears. Had someone hurt her feelings?

Behind her, the band segued into a familiar slow song and couples began flocking to the dance floor.

Phoebe swallowed and licked her lips. "I was hoping you'd dance with me tonight."

Because it was Phoebe, and because he sensed she wasn't very happy, he turned away from the exit. "All right." He took her hand and began to draw her after him to the dance floor. Whatever had upset her, he could worm it out of her while they danced.

He pulled her into the middle of the crowded area and turned to draw her into his arms. There were so many people they were literally pushed together.

Phoebe's slender body slid against his and settled as if she'd been made just for him. He realized suddenly that he'd never danced with her before. Never.

Would it have been like this between them before now if he'd been smart enough to dance with her? His heart began to pound and arousal began to stir. Automatically, he began to move to the beat of the music, and she moved with him, her soft curves a shocking temptation beneath his hands.

It was heaven. He turned his head slightly and breathed in her scent, and his entire body tightened.

What the hell… This was Phoebe. His little neighbor.

Not so little anymore. She was the same age Melanie was, though he'd bet his paycheck she was far less experienced. Stunned, confused, he actually stopped dancing right there in the middle of the crowd.

"Phoebe?" He pulled back far enough to see her face, wondering if she was feeling as overwhelmed as he was.

She tilted her head back and her entire face was shining as if someone had lit a lantern inside her. "Yes?"

When she met his eyes, something clicked into place. Something precious and irreplaceable, something that filled a spot inside him that he hadn't even realized was empty. He forgot everything he'd been going to say, everything in his head, everything in the world. Nothing else mattered because everything he needed was right here in his arms, her eyes telling him that she felt the magic they were making together as well as he.

"Never mind," he said at last. He pulled her close again, then grasped her hands, which had been resting on his shoulders, and slid them up behind his neck. The movement increased the intimacy of their position and he had to fight the urge to shift his hips against the soft body plastered to his. This was crazy. *He* was crazy. Crazy about a woman he'd known most of his life without really knowing her at all.

Phoebe made a small sound and turned her head toward him, nestling against his chest. He bent his head to hers and set his lips against her ear. "The rest of the evening."

A shiver rippled down her spine and he delighted in the knowledge that she was as aroused as he was. Her head came up and their lips were a whisper apart. "What?"

He smiled and dropped his head farther, then brushed his nose lightly across hers. He wanted to kiss her worse than he'd ever wanted anything, including his first brand new bike and his ranger tab. But when he kissed Phoebe for the first time, he didn't want an audience, and he didn't want to have to stop. "You're dancing with me for the rest of the evening."

She shot him a glowing smile, and he swore there were stars twinkling and sparkling in the depths of those blue eyes. "All right."

* * *

Dinner was the most nerve-racking experience Phoebe had ever had in her life. In the back of her head a steady cadence hammered: *I have to tell him I have to tell him I have to tell him.*

It was so insistent that she couldn't relax and enjoy these moments she'd thought were gone forever. But she couldn't tell him here, not in a restaurant.

Fortunately, Wade didn't seem to want to discuss serious topics, either. He asked about her teaching job and seemed honestly interested. He asked questions about the little house in which she lived and how she'd found it. He asked about New York and how it was different from California, but he didn't ask her why she'd moved. Thank heavens. Maybe he simply assumed that she'd wanted to get away from all the memories.

He told her a little bit about where he'd been and what he'd done. A lot of it was classified, but he could share generalities.

They didn't talk about anything important. Neither of them mentioned the reunion, or the magical moments they'd shared, or what had occurred between them after the funeral.

And they didn't talk about Melanie.

Melanie, for whom Wade had cared deeply for years before one evening of dancing…

"Phoebe, you'll never guess who's coming to the reunion with me."

"I give." She smiled as Melanie breezed into the living room of her small apartment on the weekend of their first class reunion. It had been nice to move away from home and get away from her sister, but it also was nice to see her from time to time. Melanie was lovable; she was just…too much sometimes. "Who?"

"Wade!"

Phoebe froze. She'd been expecting her sister to name a classmate, probably a male one, knowing Melanie. "Wade didn't graduate with us," she said carefully.

"I know, silly." Melanie shook her head in exasperation. "I invited him."

"But…"

"He's going to wear his uniform." Melanie waved a hand as if she was fanning herself. "I can't resist a man in uniform."

Neither could Phoebe, if that man was Wade. But she couldn't say that to Mel.

The doorbell rang then, saving her from making

a response. Melanie said, "That must be Wade. Let him in, will you? I've got to finish getting ready!"

Phoebe resisted the temptation to salute as she reluctantly moved toward the door and opened it.

"Wade." It wasn't hard to smile as she lifted her arms. It was much harder not to appear too thrilled. "It's great to see you."

"You, too." Wade's arms came around her and he kissed her lightly on the cheek before she backed away. "How've you been, Phoeber? You look terrific."

He released her and stepped back a pace. "Seriously terrific," he added, as he scanned the simple navy-blue dress she'd chosen.

"Thank you." She knew she was blushing, and not just because of the admiration in his eyes. The feel of his hard arms around her had been overwhelming to senses that had been starved for even the sight of him. To suddenly be in her version of heaven was too much. She took a deep breath. "You look good, too. The army's agreeing with you?"

He nodded. "And you're enjoying teaching." It wasn't a question; they had stayed in loose touch by e-mail once or twice a month since she'd graduated from high school and headed off to Berkeley. As badly as she longed to hear from him, Phoebe always forced herself to wait at least a week before e-mailing him back. The last thing she wanted was for Wade to realize how she felt about him.

She nodded. "I think I told you I'm switching from first grade to fourth next year. It'll be an interesting change."

He grinned. "Yeah, the boys will have gone from being mildly annoying to thoroughly bratty."

She laughed. "Hmm. Sounds like personal experience speaking."

"Fourth grade was the year I got sent to the principal's office for putting a tadpole in Miss Ladly's Thermos of iced tea."

"I've heard that story before. Guess I'll be checking before I take a sip of anything."

They smiled at each other and a companionable silence fell for a moment. But then she broke the mood. "How long are you home for, and where do you go after that?" He probably had no idea that she could recite every move he'd made in the nine years since he'd graduated from high school.

Wade's face suddenly seemed guarded, his gray eyes darkening. "I have a few more days left of my two weeks' leave and then I'm being deployed to Afghanistan."

Afghanistan. The fear she'd always lived with rose, almost choking her. "Oh, God, Wade."

"I'll be back," he said. "Who would come around to bug you once in a while if I didn't?"

She forced herself to smile. "Just be careful."

He nodded, reaching out a hand and rubbing her arm. "Thanks. I will."

"Hey there!" Her sister's voice singsonged a flirtatious greeting Phoebe had heard her employ dozens of times before. And just like many of those other times, Wade's head swiveled around and Phoebe was instantly forgotten.

Lowering her eyes, she stepped away and busied herself gathering a few items for her evening bag while Melanie threw herself into Wade's arms and gave him a loud kiss.

For the rest of the evening, she avoided looking at Wade and her sister as much as she could. It was just too painful.

Not long after they arrived at the reunion, she lost herself on the other side of the crowd. Her best friend from high school, June Nash, had come. June still lived in town. She'd married a former classmate and was expecting her first child. Phoebe felt conspicuously alone as she looked around. Everyone seemed either to be married by now or to have brought a date.

But June was genuinely delighted to see her, and they spent the mealtime catching up on the years since high school. Although they faithfully exchanged Christmas cards, their e-mails and phone calls had gradually slowed as their lives took different paths.

"So you're teaching." June smiled. "I bet you're fantastic with children. I still remember how great you were when the student council helped with Special Olympics."

Phoebe shrugged. "I enjoy it." And the school district in which she taught was far enough from where she'd grown up that few people knew her as "the quiet twin."

"That's good." June nodded her head in the direction of another group. "I see Melanie and Wade are an item again. I thought that ended a couple of years ago."

Phoebe winced. "It did. But we've all stayed friends and Melanie invited him as her date tonight."

Thankfully, the band began to play at that moment and she was spared any more discussion. June wasn't dancing since her first child was due in less than two weeks and she said she felt like a hippo in a mud hole. But a group of girls Phoebe had known when they were all in the marching band dragged her up to the dance floor with them, and Phoebe decided she was going to enjoy what was left of the evening. She danced with a group of her classmates until the first slow song and then moved to another table to visit, forbidding herself to look around the room for Wade.

An hour later, she'd had enough. She'd seen the people she'd wanted to see, had danced and laughed and done her best to give the impression that life was treating Phoebe Merriman well. Melanie, as always, was the life of the party. She had abandoned Wade for a guy Phoebe barely remembered, and the two of them were knocking back drinks with a like-minded group.

This time Phoebe did look for Wade. He was standing alone by the bar and, as she watched, he set down his drink and approached Melanie. After a brief exchange, Melanie laughed and Wade turned and walked away.

When she realized he was heading for the door, she panicked. Plain and simple, she couldn't bear the thought of Wade leaving without at least speaking to him one more time.

"Wade!" she called out. "Wait!"

Two little words. She could still remember them. Two little words that had altered her life. And not just hers. Three lives had been altered by that evening, four if you counted Bridget. If Wade had left the dance when he'd intended to, Melanie might still be alive. If Melanie were still alive,

Phoebe and Wade would never have walked up to that cabin, would never have...and Bridget would never have been conceived.

Try as she might, Phoebe couldn't regret those stolen moments of heaven she'd experienced with him. Nor could she imagine her world without her beautiful baby daughter in it.

"Would you like to go to a movie when we're finished eating?" Wade smiled at her across the table. A movie. With Wade.

There was a time when she would have given an arm for that invitation. But things were different now. What she wanted and what was reality were two very separate things.

"Thank you, but no," she said. "I have to get home pretty soon."

He looked taken aback and, as she watched, the warmth in his eyes drained away. "All right."

"Wade." She leaned forward and took an irrevocable step. "I'd like you to come with me. There's something I have to tell you."

"You mentioned that yesterday," he said, but she noticed he seemed to unbend a little. "Sounds scary."

She couldn't even smile. "I hope not."

They left the restaurant and he followed her minivan directly back to her house. She'd offer him a glass of wine first, she decided, and then...

then she'd have to decide how to tell him. But none of her opening lines sounded good. And now she had a new worry.

What if Wade didn't want to be a father? What if he rejected Bridget and didn't want to be part of her life?

Since yesterday, Phoebe had been trying to brace herself for sharing Bridget with her father when he came East. Which could be quite infrequently. After all, the man was probably going to be out of the country most of the time. If Wade didn't want anything to do with them, their lives wouldn't change appreciably.

But it would break her heart if he didn't find Bridget as miraculous and irresistible as she did.

He followed her into the house at her invitation.

And it was then that she realized the flaw in her plan. Duh. How could she possibly explain the presence of a nanny?

Angie rose from the couch and gathered up her schoolwork. "Hi, Phoebe. Give me a minute to get organized and call my brother. I have an econ test tomorrow."

Phoebe managed a smile. "Do you think you're ready?"

Angie shrugged. "As ready as I'll ever be."

She glanced at the ceiling. "Everything went fine this evening."

Phoebe was having trouble getting out words. Her chest felt like there was an enormous weight bearing down, preventing her from taking one good, deep breath. "Good."

Angie nodded and went to the phone. A moment later, she said, "He's on his way."

"I'll walk out with you." One more minute. Just one more minute to plan what she was going to say. Her hands were shaking as she followed the sitter to the end of her driveway. Angie's brother was already rounding the corner and walking toward them, and Phoebe returned his wave as Angie moved away.

Then she took one last stab at a deep breath and turned toward her home again.

Wade stood framed in the doorway. His face was in the shadow, and golden light from her cozy little home streamed around him, illuminating the tall, unmoving figure. It looked right, she thought. Then she immediately censored the notion. There was no point in wishing for the moon.

Phoebe mounted the steps and he moved aside to let her enter. His brow furrowed as he watched her close the door behind herself. "You have a housekeeper?"

"No." She took a deep breath. "No, I don't. Angela is my nanny." It wasn't, perhaps, a perfect opening line, but she might as well jump in. She had to get this over with.

She watched the expressions move swiftly across his face: simple acceptance of an answer, then shock, and a growing incredulity as he took in what she had said. "Why do you have a nanny?" He looked around as if to confirm the obvious conclusion, but the books and toys had been put away in the large basket beneath the window, so there was no obvious evidence of a child in residence in the living room.

"I have a daughter."

"I see." His expression had gone so noncommittal she wondered what in the world he was thinking. Of all the reactions, calm acceptance wasn't the one she'd anticipated.

"Wade?"

To her shock, he had started for the door. "This was a mistake," he said. "Goodbye, Phoebe."

"Wade!"

He stopped halfway to the door without turning around. "Yeah?"

"Don't you even want to know about her?"

There was a long moment in which she held her breath. Then he turned around and in his eyes she saw a sadness so deep she couldn't fathom what was wrong. Surely the existence of a child couldn't be that terrible, could it? Maybe it reminded him of what he would never have with Melanie—

"No," he finally said. "I don't."

"But—"

"What we did—after the funeral—meant something to me."

And she had known it would. He'd had a sense of honor a mile wide as long as she'd known him. It was one of the reasons she had been so loath to tell him she was pregnant. Even after she'd gotten past the hurt and the anger that he'd never contacted her after what they'd shared, she'd feared his reaction. She knew Wade well. He would have felt obligated to ask her to marry him.

The last thing she wanted was a man who felt forced into a loveless marriage with his child's mother. But dear Lord, if he'd asked her to marry him then…she wasn't sure she'd have had the strength to turn him down.

"I assumed it meant something to you," he added.

"It did!" He was the first and only man she'd ever been with. He couldn't possibly know what that meant to her.

"But you've moved on." He laughed, but it wasn't a sound of humor. "You've moved on in a big way."

She couldn't follow.... "I didn't have a choice," she said.

"Is the father still in the picture? I presume you're not married or you wouldn't have gone out with me tonight. I hope," he said coolly.

She blinked, completely thrown off stride. He thought she'd—he thought Bridget was—"No," she said. "You don't understand. There is no other man."

"Maybe not now, but—"

"She's yours."

Three

Wade froze, his face a classic mask of disbelief. Finally, as if he were sure he hadn't understood what language she was speaking, he said, "What?"

"She's your child," Phoebe said. She probably should have been angry at his initial assumption that there'd been another man, but he looked so totally poleaxed now that she couldn't summon much outrage.

"Are you kidding me?" He sounded as shocked as he looked. "We only—that one time—"

She nodded sympathetically, understanding his shock. "That's how I felt when I found out, too."

"When you found out." He pounced on that like a cat waiting for the mouse to come out just far enough, shock morphing into anger right before her eyes. "Just when in the hell *did* you find out? And why didn't you bother to tell me?"

She forced herself not to stammer apologetically. Instead, she indicated the couch. "Would you like to sit down? I'll explain it all."

"Hell, no, I don't want to sit down!" The words exploded with fury. "I just want to know why you didn't tell me you were going to have a baby!"

She wanted to shrink into a little ball and hide beneath the furniture, exactly like a frightened mouse. The guilt she had lived with since his death flared to life. "I don't know," she said in a quiet voice. "At the time, it seemed like the thing to do. Now— for some time now—I've known it was wrong."

"So why didn't you look me up and tell me?"

"You were dead! At least, I thought you were."

He fell silent, clearly taken aback. "I keep forgetting that," he said in a slightly milder tone. Then his eyes narrowed. "But I wasn't dead when you found out you were pregnant."

She had to look away. "No," she said, "you weren't."

Silence fell. She wrapped her arms around

herself and turned away, feeling the rage crackling in the room behind her.

"I want to see her," he said.

"All right." She swallowed. "Tomorrow after school—"

"*Now.*" The word was a whip and she jumped as it lashed her ears.

"She's asleep," she said protectively. But Wade's face was stony and unmoved when she looked back at him. "All right." She blew out a breath of nerves and exasperation, realizing she'd been stupid to imagine she could tell Wade about his child without letting him see her for himself immediately. "I'll take you up to see her if you promise not to wake her."

There was another tense silence. Finally, Wade said, "So let's go."

She turned on her heel and walked to the stairs on shaking legs, leaving him to follow.

She was extremely aware of his large presence at her back as she went up the steps and down the hall. At the door of her daughter's room, she paused. Her chest felt as if someone were sitting on it and she couldn't get enough air. She'd swear she could feel Wade's breath on the back of her neck and she didn't have the courage to turn around. Over her shoulder, she whispered, "Her name is Bridget. She's six months old."

The door was open just a shred, and she grasped the knob and carefully pulled it wide, then stepped aside and gestured. "Go ahead."

Wade nodded once, a sharp jerk of his head, and she watched from the doorway as he took slow, almost hesitant steps toward the crib against the far wall.

He stood there for a long, long time, looking down at the sleeping baby in the low light she'd switched on. He didn't move to touch her, didn't glance around the room at the charming wallpaper border with the red-and-blue alphabet-blocks motif she'd found, the gingham curtains or the shelves filled with board books, stuffed animals and toys to stimulate a growing baby. He just… stood.

Finally, she entered the room and went to his side.

"Is she really mine?" His low voice was wondering and she understood he wasn't trying to offend her.

"She's really yours," she assured him softly. "You can touch her." His big hands were still, grasping the rail of the crib. He made no move but Phoebe could practically feel the longing radiating from him. Finally, she couldn't stand it. She took his hand, and when he didn't resist, she lifted it and tugged him forward so his palm rested flat against Bridget's small back.

Phoebe found she had a lump in her throat. Her daughter's body looked so tiny and fragile with Wade's hand covering her whole back.

Her own hand tingled where she'd touched his skin. It wasn't fair. Even an innocent touch like that set her pulse racing. In the years before and after Wade, she'd never met another man who could affect her so effortlessly. She doubted he even knew he'd done it.

But she knew. For the rest of her life, she'd always be comparing any man she met to Wade. She hoped to marry someday, but she was realistic enough to know that she wasn't going to be able to offer a man the kind of all-consuming love she felt for Wade. She also knew she could never pretend to care for someone just to get a ring on her finger, and she feared that there might be many lonely years in her future, broken up by the joys of motherhood.

She was distracted from her morose thoughts by movement. Bridget had squirmed and twitched in her sleep, and Wade had automatically soothed her with gentle circles on her back. The baby gave a sigh and stopped moving, but he didn't. He extended his index finger and very, very lightly brushed it over the smooth petal softness of his daughter's cheek. He stroked it back and forth over the wild red curls that sprang from her tiny head. Then his hand moved to touch her much smaller one.

And Phoebe thought her heart might break when Bridget grasped one big finger and held on for dear life, still sound asleep. A lump rose in her throat and she fought not to sob aloud at the tenderness of the moment.

She swallowed hard several times until she felt she had enough control not to cry. Then she opened her mouth to whisper an apology, but when her gaze landed on his face, the words dried up in her throat.

Wade had tears on his cheeks. Silvery in the moonlight, they made gleaming trails where they fell from his eyes and rolled down his face. He didn't even seem to notice them, not even when one fat tear dripped from his jaw onto the back of the hand that still clutched the side of the crib.

His sorrow hit her harder than anything in the world had since the news of his death. And guilt was right on its heels. *She* was the cause of this agony. *She* was the source of the sadness that gripped him. She hadn't told him about her pregnancy when she'd had the chance, and then she'd lost the chance, she'd thought, forever.

Wade turned away from the crib and made his way from the room slowly. She followed him equally slowly, her own battle with tears completely lost. As they moved down the hallway, she swallowed the sob that wanted to surge up and said, "Wade, I—"

"Don't." He held up one large hand in a gesture of denial without even turning around. "I can't talk to you right now," he said as he started down the steps.

Shaken by both his tears and the controlled ferocity in the low tone, Phoebe stopped talking.

And watched, stunned, as Wade walked out the front door of her home without another word.

Wade knew she went to work the next day because he was sitting in his parked car down the street, waiting for her to come home. When she emerged from her little minivan, she walked around to the passenger-side sliding door and unloaded what looked like a fifty-pound satchel, presumably full of work to be graded.

The sight of Phoebe lugging that obviously heavy load up her front steps aroused two emotions in him. The first was an instinctive protective urge. She shouldn't be lifting things like that. The second was another blast of the anger that had consumed him since last night, when it had fully begun to sink in that he had a child—and had missed more than half a year of her life because Phoebe had chosen to deny him the knowledge of his fatherhood. He didn't even know his child's birthday but he could guess approximately when she had been born.

God, if only Phoebe had told him when she'd learned she was pregnant…it might have made all the difference in the world.

He'd have married her. Hell, he'd known he wanted to marry her since they'd danced together at her class reunion and he'd realized what had been right under his nose for years. But then Mel was killed and things had gotten more and more out of control after that.

She'd been extremely drunk and upset that night and it had been his fault. The thought would haunt him forever, and he knew it had to have occurred to Phoebe. He could have stopped her from drinking so much. He could have gone after her faster. God, was it any wonder Phoebe hadn't wanted to contact him when she'd found out she was pregnant? If she blamed him for Melanie's death, how must she feel about having slept with him the very day of her twin's funeral?

He took deep, calming breaths as he got out of his

rental car and strode along the sidewalk to her house. A twinge in his hip reminded him that he wasn't quite as healthy as he wanted to be just yet. He had to get a grip. Yes, she'd been wrong, but shouting at her wasn't going to help the situation any.

Even if it would make him feel one hell of a lot better.

The door had barely closed behind her when he turned into her walk and bounded up the steps. He rapped briskly on the door.

Phoebe pulled it open a moment later. "Yes? Wade!" She clearly hadn't expected it to be him. Maybe she'd thought he'd gone back to California. *Think again.*

He stepped across the threshold, forcing her to step back. Her babysitter was just getting ready to slip out the door but she paused, brown eyes alight with interest.

"Bye, Angie." Phoebe held the door open and waved a hand, ushering the younger woman out. "See you Monday. Have a good weekend." The nanny was barely through the door when Phoebe closed it behind her. Then she turned to face him. "Hello. Would you like to come in?"

He snorted at her sarcasm, but he'd been thinking all night and he wanted to get things straight right from the get-go. "Okay. The way I see it, we have two choices. We go back to California, or we stay here."

Her blue eyes widened to the size of saucers. "*We? You* can do whatever you like but—"

"I'd like to take my daughter back to California to meet her only surviving grandparent," he said harshly.

Her lovely face registered horrified shock. "You can't just take off with my child."

"No, but I can take off with my child," he said.

He could see the moment that his earlier words registered. Phoebe's forehead wrinkled and her eyes widened as she said, "One grandparent? Wade, has one of your parents passed away?"

"My mother." Anger was preferable by far to the grief that still gripped him at unexpected times. "She died seven months ago."

"Oh, my God." Phoebe looked stunned. Her eyes filled with tears. "I need to sit down." Her voice was faint and she stepped backward until the couch hit the backs of her knees. Then she collapsed onto the cushion, her hands clasped together so tightly he could see her knuckles whiten. "Oh, Wade, I'm so sorry. What happened?"

"She had a stroke," he said flatly. "Ten months ago. It was terribly debilitating and she didn't want to live. Three months after the first one, she had another." *But if she'd known she'd had a grand-child, things might have been different.* He could see in Phoebe's horrified eyes that the thought had occurred to her as well.

She pressed the heels of her hands hard against her eyes, elbows resting on her thighs. "I am so sorry," she said in a muffled voice.

He knew she wasn't offering condolences. No, she was apologizing—again—for not telling him he had a child. "I want Dad to meet Bridget," he said, "before much more time passes."

"But...I can't just quit my job and go off to California."

"I didn't ask you to," he said evenly.

Phoebe's face lost what little color it still had. "Are you...are you going to fight me for custody?"

He took his time answering, finding himself a seat in the comfortable armchair angled close to the sofa. "Are you going to force me to?" He waited until she met his gaze. "I want to get to know my daughter. I want to be with her every day—I can't get back all the time I missed but I sure as hell don't want to miss any more." He closed his eyes against the surge of anger that shook him and waited for her to argue.

"Okay." Her voice was small.

He was startled. "Okay?" The Phoebe he knew

might be quiet and calm, but underneath she was a fighter when she believed in something.

But she nodded. "Okay." She swallowed. "I was wrong not to tell you as soon as I found out, Wade. I'm sorrier than you'll ever know."

He didn't know what to say to that. She was right—she had been wrong. Because she'd chosen not to tell him, his mother had died without ever knowing she had a grandchild.

He simply couldn't utter the words to accept her apology yet. He liked to think he was a big enough man that he'd soon be able to forgive her... but he didn't feel that magnanimous right now. Instead of answering, he stood and went out the front door to his car.

When he returned, Phoebe was still sitting on the couch with her hands clasped. She jumped up when he walked back in without knocking and dumped his duffel on the floor inside the door. There were tears on her face, which she hastily wiped away, and then she did a double take.

"What are you doing?" She already knew, and she was aghast.

"Moving in." He shrugged. "It's the only way to really get to know Bridget without taking her away from you."

She nodded as if she saw the logic, but a

moment later, she shook her head vigorously. "Wait! You can't just move in here!"

"Why not? You and I have always gotten along well. We probably know each other better than a lot of couples do. And you have an extra bedroom. I saw it last night. I'll pay rent."

She opened her mouth, then closed it again and shook her head helplessly. Finally, she said, "This is outrageous. So how did you just make it sound so utterly logical?"

He grinned, feeling a lot more relaxed now that she hadn't kicked him out first thing. "I'm gifted that way." He'd hoped her obvious guilt would help sway her to his point of view and, apparently, it had worked.

Suddenly, he realized she hadn't spoken. She was staring at him as if he'd grown a second head. "What?"

She shrugged. "That's the first time I've seen you smile since you got off that swing yesterday."

"I haven't had much to smile about," he pointed out.

Instantly, the angry tension was back in the room, humming between them like a downed electrical wire. He was about to speak again, to get more answers to the questions she'd never given him a chance to ask, when an odd whispering sound filled the air.

It was barely audible, but Phoebe reacted instantly, a blinding smile lighting her face. "Bridget is awake."

His body reacted to that smile. But—

"A-ba-bah-bah-ba," It was a little louder now. Wade glanced around the room and spotted a baby monitor on one end table. Aha.

Phoebe started for the stairs. "If I don't get her fast, they'll hear her down at the end of the street. I'll be back in a minute."

Wade smiled to himself as she took the steps two at a time. Bridget was six months old. That had to be a bit of an exaggeration—

"A-bah-bah-BAH-BAH!"

Whoa. His kid had a set of lungs on her like Pavarotti.

"Bridget." Phoebe's voice was a gentle singsong. "How's my girl? Did you have a good nap?"

The baby gave a delighted squeal that just about split his eardrums. Did Phoebe have that monitor turned up too high?

"Hello, my sweet baby girl." No, the monitor wasn't too loud, because Phoebe's voice sounded normal. "How was your nap? I've got somebody downstairs who wants to meet you." He heard her chuckle. "But first we'd better change your diaper or he's liable to keel over."

He listened to the rustle of the plastic diaper and the baby cooing, to Phoebe talking and singing little nonsense verses. It sounded surprisingly *right*. But he shouldn't be surprised. Phoebe had always had a sensible, motherly streak. Years ago, if someone had asked him if he could envision her as a mother, he wouldn't have hesitated for an instant before saying yes.

A wave of intense sadness swamped him. And now she was the mother of his child. If he hadn't been determined to find Phoebe, he'd never even have known he had a daughter.

Footsteps on the stairs alerted him that they were coming, and he shook off the moment of melancholy and braced himself for his first clear sight of his daughter. He knew from what he'd seen last night that her hair was some shade of red, but the low light of the nursery hadn't yielded much more.

Phoebe's legs came into view, and then the rest of her appeared. She was carrying a baby girl with the wildest red hair he'd ever seen in his life. Quirking in ringlets all over her head. Even at this young age, Phoebe had pulled the front of it atop her head with an elastic hair tie. Bridget's hair was much lighter than Phoebe's, and far more vibrant than Melanie's pale strawberry had ever been. His kid's hair looked like a live flame.

Her face was a pretty little oval with a slightly more determined chin than was probably good, her eyes blue and sparkling as they found him. His heart skipped a beat. He actually *felt* it trip and miss, and he took a deep breath. God, she looked a lot like Phoebe.

His throat closed up and he just stood there as they approached. Phoebe was talking to the baby as if she could understand every word she said, telling her about a friend of Mama's from far away who was coming to stay with them for a little while.

A little while? Ha. She might not choose to accept it, but he was here for good.

He swallowed the thick knot clogging his voice. "Hi, Bridget," he said. He was at a loss. What did you say to somebody this size?

The child grinned, a wide smile that sent a cascade of drool down her chin and showed him two tiny pearly white teeth on the bottom. Then she turned her head abruptly into her mother's shoulder.

Before he could figure out what to say, Phoebe saved him. "Daddy," she told his child. "Bridget, this is your daddy."

The baby peeked out at him with one blue eye, then grinned before hiding her face again.

"Flirt," said Phoebe. She walked across the room and expertly unfurled a large baby blanket while still holding the child on her hip with the other hand. Then she set the baby in the middle of the blanket.

Bridget wobbled for a moment, then seemed to find her balance and sit straighter. "She just started sitting up by herself two weeks ago," she told Wade over her shoulder. "Why don't you come sit down and play with us? She's not usually shy and she should get used to you quickly."

"All right." He strove for a normal tone although his heart felt as if it were going to fly right out of his chest.

He joined them on the brightly colored blanket. Phoebe was building a tower of blocks. Every time she'd get three or four stacked up, Bridget swiped her hand and knocked them over, squealing and chortling. Once, when Phoebe stopped for a moment, the baby smacked her little hands together and yelled, "Ack!" in a tone that left no doubt what she wanted.

Wade hastily reached for another block. "Way to get what you want, kid."

Phoebe chuckled. "She has a mind of her own. And if she doesn't get her way, she lets me know about it."

"Reminds me of Melanie." He'd said it without thinking. The moment the words hit the air, he knew they'd been a mistake.

The happiness drained out of Phoebe's eyes, leaving them guarded and sorrowful. "Yes," she said quietly. "Bridget does seem to have a stronger personality than I ever had."

He wanted to protest. There was nothing wrong with Phoebe's personality. Just because Mel had been more vocal about everything under the sun didn't mean Phoebe's personality was any less pleasing. She just wasn't loud and attention-grabbing, that was all. But he didn't know how to say that in a way that made much sense, and he could almost feel the resistance in the air. She didn't want to talk about Melanie, that much was clear.

A pang of guilt shot through him, tempering the anger that still simmered. He was blaming Phoebe for not telling him about the baby…but he'd been responsible for her sister's death. No wonder she hadn't told him.

The baby had grabbed a board book and was busily manhandling the sturdy pages. As he watched, she put it in her mouth.

"Here, honey." Phoebe extended a brightly colored set of rings and confiscated the book. "We don't chew on books."

Wade looked at the frayed corners of the one she held. "Apparently, some of us do."

She smiled, and abruptly it felt right between them again. "I'm working on it," she said wryly. Then she glanced at her watch. "It'll soon be dinnertime. Would you like to stay and eat with us?"

He raised one eyebrow.

"Are you planning to stay here *tonight?*"

"That's the plan." He stood and folded his arms. "If you spend the weekend teaching me how to take care of Bridget, then I could keep her while you work."

"Don't you have to work or something?" she asked in an exasperated tone.

"Or something," he agreed.

"So you have to go back to California." It wasn't a question.

"No. I'm pretty sure I'm retiring from the service."

She looked shocked. "But that's what you've always wanted to do. To be. A soldier."

"I'm not physically able to perform on the battlefield to the army's satisfaction anymore," he said quietly. "And I'm not interested in a desk job staring at a computer monitor all day. So I'm taking early retirement."

"But what will you do?"

He shrugged. "I'm checking out a number of options. One of them is with a freelance security firm out of Virginia. I'd be establishing a West Coast office."

"So you'd be going home?"

He noted with satisfaction that she still referred to California as home. But all he did was nod. "That would be the plan." He shrugged. "But now, everything has changed." He looked down at his daughter, who had rolled onto her stomach and was making swimming motions as she tried valiantly to get to another toy just out of reach. "Everything."

Four

Phoebe still sat on the blanket at Wade's feet and he reached down, putting his hands beneath her elbows and lifting her to her feet.

Her eyes were fastened on his face; her hands fell to rest against his chest for a moment before she moved away. She cleared her throat. "I understand it's going to take some time to get used to being a father," she told him, indicating the baby playing at their feet. Her voice was huskier than normal.

His body was having no trouble understanding that the woman he'd dreamed of for months—hell, years—was standing practically in his arms. *The mother of his child.* The anger he'd been hiding couldn't be summoned. Instead, he found the thought surprisingly arousing. Here, right before them, was something they'd made together during those wild, impossibly wonderful moments they'd shared in the cabin.

He exerted a little pressure until she stopped resisting and let him draw her forward. "It's amazing that we created that."

She nodded, looking straight ahead at his throat rather than tilting her head back. "It's a miracle."

He pressed a feather light kiss against her temple and felt her body shudder. "I'm still pissed at you. But thank you."

"I, ah—I don't think—"

"Don't think," he urged. "I won't if you won't."

He wanted to kiss her. He'd dreamed of it for so long that he could hardly believe this was real. Releasing her wrist, he put one finger beneath her chin and lifted her face to his. "Kiss me," he said. "Relax and let me—ahhh." In unison, they made an involuntary sound of pure pleasure as his thighs pressed into the cradle of her hips and his hardening body nudged the tender flesh between her legs.

He couldn't wait anymore. He dropped his head and fastened his mouth on hers, kissing her hard and deep, pouring all the longing and frustration of the past two years into the embrace. He felt her hands clench on his shoulders, but she wasn't pushing him away. Oh, no. He felt the way she melted against him, the way her fingers dug into his flesh and he knew she was going to be his again. But this time, he promised himself, he wasn't going to be a cad, wasn't going to leave her without a word.

This was a dream, Phoebe thought. It had to be. She'd imagined Wade kissing her so many times in the past year that it felt unreal to have him here, holding her against him. His tongue demanded her response, his big arms molded her close to the lean strength of his body. His state of arousal was impossible to miss, plastered against him as she was.

And memory rushed in, recalling the other time they'd been in this kind of embrace....

She was in heaven.

Phoebe nestled her face into Wade's throat and felt him shudder as they danced. This was a dream. It had to be. But oh, what a dream. She never wanted to wake up.

"Hey, you." She felt Wade's lips move against her forehead.

She lifted her head and smiled up into his gray eyes. Even in the low light on the dance floor, they seemed to blaze with heat and desire. For her? She was definitely dreaming.

"I want to take you home tonight." His voice was rough. "But I can't. You've got the car."

"You can drive," she offered. "Since we're practically going to the same place."

"I wish we were going home together," he said. "I'd like to hold you all night long."

His frank words were shocking, in a knot-in-the-belly exciting kind of way, and she knew her eyes widened.

"I don't want to rush you," he said quickly. "I realize this is new—"

"It's not new for me," she broke in. She reached up and placed a soft palm against his cheek. "Wade, don't you know I've—" loved you "—wanted this for a long time?"

He placed his hand over hers, holding it in place as he turned his head and pressed a hot kiss into her palm. He closed his eyes briefly. "I'm a dope. I never realized—"

"Shh. It's okay." She didn't want him to feel bad, or awkward, about anything. "Let's just start from this night."

"That sounds like a solid plan to me." He

smiled. Then his hand slid down, freeing hers as he cupped her chin and lifted her face to his.

She caught her breath, sure he was about to kiss her. Oh, God, she would melt right into the floor if he did—

"What's going on here?" The voice was strident, female, furious—and familiar.

Phoebe jolted, tearing herself free from Wade's arms.

Melanie stood in front of them, hands fisted on her hips. "Thanks for taking such good care of *my date,* sister dear," she said in a taut, sarcastic voice.

"Back off, Mel." Wade's voice was cool and commanding. "You didn't even notice I was leaving. Why the scene now?"

"Wade." Melanie turned luminous blue eyes on him and, instantly, the anger vanished and tears welled. "You—you brought me to the reunion. Why would you treat me this way?"

Wade shook his head. "Save the act for somebody who buys it. You couldn't have cared less what Phoebe and I were doing—"

"Phoebe and you." Anger distorted Melanie's pretty features and she tossed her long, shining hair back. Her eyes narrowed as she focused on Phoebe. "Sneaking around behind my back. My own sister. My twin. You've always wanted him, haven't you?

You've been in love with him the whole time, but he was mine."

"That's enough." Wade took Melanie's elbow, but she shook him off. Around them, people had stopped dancing and were staring openly, watching the drama unfold.

And Melanie loved it, Phoebe knew. She was the quintessential drama queen. This act was perfect for her.

"No," Melanie said, and her voice grew shrill. "That's not nearly enough. I will never forgive you for this, Wade. And you." She stabbed an angry finger in Phoebe's direction. "I wish I never had to see you again!"

And with one final toss of her bright tresses, Melanie whirled and stomped away, fury radiating from every move. The only thing that spoiled it was that she'd had far too much to drink and she staggered as she headed for the door, jostling a gaping group of classmates. "Get out of my way," she shrieked. She had worked herself into a sobbing fit of tears by that time.

Wade turned back to Phoebe. "We'd better go after her. She's had way too much to drink."

"Yes." She nodded. "It's a good thing she doesn't have a car."

"Come with me." He held out a hand.

She shook her head, her throat clogged with sobs. "No. She'll be impossible if she sees me. You know she'll calm down if she doesn't see us together."

Wade nodded, letting his hand drop to his side as he acknowledged the truth of her statement.

She turned and walked to the table where her small evening bag lay. "Here." She extended her car keys. "You take her home. I'll catch a ride later."

Wade took the keys. Then he caught her hand with his free one, bringing it to his lips for a moment. "I'll call you," he said.

Her heart leaped at the tender gesture. Could he really mean it? Could this evening, the moments between them on the dance floor, really be the day she'd dreamed of since she was old enough to feel her heart beating faster in his presence?

She offered him a shaky smile. "I'll look forward to it," she said, clutching the promise to her heart as he started away.

Just then, they heard tires shrieking in the parking lot.

"What the hell…?" Wade began to run full-out.

Phoebe rushed after him. She reached the door just in time to see her car flying out of the parking lot and down the road, and she knew immediately what had happened. Melanie knew Phoebe kept a spare key in a magnetic box in the wheel well. She'd taken the car.

Phoebe tore her mouth from Wade's. "This isn't— we can't do this." She was embarrassed that she was practically panting. And then she realized that she had a death grip on his wide shoulders. And worse, she'd made no move to separate their bodies, which were stuck like two slices of the peanut butter bread she often slapped together for lunch.

Wade's eyebrows rose. There was a glint in his eye that looked almost dangerous. "We just did."

"Anymore," she tacked on belatedly, removing her hands and stepping back, forcing him to release her.

"Ever?"

"Ever."

"Because…"

"Because your life is in California—" she spread her hands "—or wherever, and mine is here in New York now."

"Mine won't be wherever anymore," he informed her. "I'm going to live here if that's where you two will be. It's not half-bad."

"It gets really cold in the winter."

"I lived at West Point for four years, remember? Believe me, I know how cold it gets here."

"You always said you wanted to live somewhere warm," she reminded him.

"Being around for my daughter is a lot more important than worrying about the temperature. So your reasoning doesn't hold. What else is bothering you?"

"Well… It isn't fair of you to spring this on me without giving me a chance to think about it." *I can't get involved with him.*

Why? He wanted you after the funeral. And before, at the dance.

Wanting isn't love.

It's a start.

No false hope, she lectured herself. *He wanted to teach Mel a lesson at the reunion. It wasn't his fault she'd flown off the handle and everything had gone so horribly wrong. And the other… What guy's going to say no when a woman pretty much tears his clothes off and has her way with him?*

"Take your time. I'm listening."

But he wasn't. His eyes were on Bridget, watching her every move with an intensity that was painful to see. It was obvious he'd forgotten all about the kiss.

Bridget was happily oblivious. She was still lying on the floor with the toy she'd finally managed to snag. She rolled over on her back and was vigorously shaking it so that a musical chime sounded inside.

"She entertains herself well for her age." Phoebe glanced at her watch, trying to keep her voice from quavering. It tore at her heart to see Wade so desperately interested in his child. "But any minute now she's going to realize that it's snack time."

Friendly. Neighborly. That was the ticket. She could ignore her temporary lapse in judgment if she just concentrated on remembering Wade several years earlier as he'd been before—before anything had happened. They'd been friends. No reason they couldn't continue to be friends.

Wade still wasn't looking at her although she had a feeling he knew exactly why she'd changed the subject. But he didn't object, merely followed her cue. "Won't a snack spoil her dinner?"

"Not if it's a small snack like a cracker. And we don't usually eat until close to six." And then they'd sit down to dinner together, just like a real family.

A real family? What was she thinking? They were *not* a family. They were two people who had known each other for a long time and who now shared a child. But they hadn't shared most of the other basic details that members of a real family would have.

And they might not be a real family, but they certainly were going to be doing many of the things that families did. Her best bet, she decided, was to treat him as a tenant. Or no, maybe a boarder… he'd already announced he was moving in, so they were going to have to handle all the dumb little details, like meals and who bought toilet paper.

And there was the fact that they hadn't really talked about custody or visitation or any of the much bigger issues that had been haunting her all day. "I have to get dinner organized," she said, knowing she sounded less than gracious. "Nothing fancy, just a roast I put in the Crock-Pot this morning."

"I love red meat. It doesn't have to be fancy." He said it with a straight face and perfectly innocent eyes. Was she only imagining the double entendre?

She felt her face slowly heating and she turned away before he could see her blushing. "I'll make dinner if you'd like to play with Bridget."

"What do you do with her when you're alone?"

"She comes into the kitchen with me. I used to put her in an infant seat and sing to her but recently I've been able to lay a blanket down and let her roll around on it."

"She looks like you." He was watching Bridget again.

"Until she decides she wants something. When she's determined, she sets her jaw the same way you do, and her eyes get that intense look."

"I do not set my jaw."

Phoebe smiled. "Okay. I must have imagined it about a million times in the last twenty years."

He had to chuckle at that. "You know me well." The amusement faded from his eyes. "And that's another reason I need to be in Bridget's life. She deserves to know how her parents met, that we grew up together."

How her parents met? He made it sound as if they were an old married couple. That thought hurt. Hurt enough that she couldn't face him anymore, and she walked away without looking back. But when she reached the kitchen door and she did glance his way again, Wade was still standing there eyeing her with a speculative expression that made her very, very wary. She knew what he'd said about not fighting over Bridget… but could she trust him?

She watched him walk over and lower himself to the floor, tailor-fashion. He was incredibly limber for such a big man. Any man, really.

Bridget turned toward him with a delighted smile as he picked her up and set her in his lap. She promptly grabbed his finger and dragged it into her mouth.

Wade looked at Phoebe over his shoulder with a pained expression. A chuckle bubbled up and nearly escaped, and she couldn't help smiling as she moved into the kitchen. He was the one who'd wanted to get to know his daughter.

But she sobered rapidly as she checked the roast. Dear heaven, what was she doing? She couldn't just give in and let Wade live in her house!

But she didn't have a choice. If she didn't let him have free access to Bridget, he'd go to a lawyer.

In her heart, she knew she could never fight him on the issue, anyway. She felt terrible for keeping her pregnancy from him, worse that she'd never told him about his child. Guilt would kill her if she denied him one moment of time with his child.

And she'd never forgive herself for not telling him—or his family, when she'd thought he was gone forever—and letting his mother die without ever knowing she had a granddaughter.

Even if he'd been dead, as she'd assumed, she should have gone to his parents. She knew it, and she knew it was part of the anger that leaped in his eyes each time he dropped the carefully friendly facade.

She shivered as she assembled ingredients for biscuit dough and got out broccoli. He would never forgive her for that. Never.

The kid was a ball of fire. He sat on the floor of his daughter's bedroom later that evening, listening to the sounds of her bath progressing. He wondered who was wetter, Phoebe or the kid. Bridget made noise nonstop, giggling, squealing and occasionally shouting. In the background, intermittent splashing indicated that the bath wasn't quite over yet.

A few moments later, he heard Phoebe's footsteps in the hallway. She stopped in the doorway to the bedroom, the baby in her arms.

Bridget was wrapped in some kind of white towel with a hood, and she sent him a cheery smile that showed her two front teeth. Phoebe set her down beside him, and her diaper made a funny plastic hiss when she plopped down on the carpet. She immediately began waving her little arms, opening and closing her fingers, her babbling beginning to escalate in pitch until Phoebe snatched up a book and thrust it into her hands. Bridget squealed, a sound so high-pitched that it made him wince.

Yep, definitely a ball of fire.

And he meant that almost literally, Wade decided, eyeing the brilliant curls, still damp from her bath, that peeped out from beneath the edges of the white terry cloth on her head.

"Time to get you into your pajamas, little miss." Phoebe came over and sank down beside them holding a set of pink pajamas. "Here," she said to

Wade. "If you want to keep her next week, you'd better start practicing how to get baby clothes on and off. Sometimes I think the manufacturers sit around and brainstorm ways to confuse parents. Hey, c'mere, you." She deftly snagged the baby, who had begun to roll out of reach. "Oh, no you don't. It's bedtime."

Bedtime.

If someone had told him he'd be sleeping under the same roof with Phoebe two days after he'd flown east, he'd have figured they were nuts.

Bedtime. Phoebe.

How the hell was he going to sleep knowing she was right in the next room?

His daughter screeched as Phoebe set her in front of him again. "Go for it," she said, smiling.

"You're going to enjoy this, aren't you?"

"Oh, yeah." She chuckled. "I had to learn by doing, so it's only fair that you have the same experience."

"Thanks." He picked up the pajamas. There were snaps in places he didn't even know snaps could be sewn. And his hands were about twice the size of the little piece of clothing. This was going to be interesting. To his relief, Phoebe returned to the dresser from which the pajamas had come and began putting away items from a clothes basket set atop it.

Twenty minutes later, he breathed a sigh of relief. "There. I think that's it."

She came over and knelt beside him to look, then raised her gaze to his and nodded. "You got it. You pass Clothing the Baby 101."

He snorted. "What's 102?"

"Well, 102," she said, "is the class where you learn the Murphy's Laws of Childrearing. Like, 'a child does not have to go to the potty until after you have completely zipped, buttoned and snapped every loose fastener on a snowsuit.'"

"Sounds like you already know them."

"Teaching," she said, "has taught me at least as much as I've taught my students. Which reminds me, no school tomorrow. It's Saturday," Phoebe said. "Bridget's not much for sleeping in so we'll be up anytime after six or so."

"Six! You're kidding. I'm on leave."

She shook her head. "No such thing when you're a parent."

"I'll get up with her if you'd like to sleep in."

Phoebe looked at him as if he'd spoken another language. "You'd do that?"

"Well, sure. It must be tough being the one on call every minute of every day."

"It's not so bad." Her tone was stiff, as if he'd offended her. "You're welcome to get up with us," she said, "but until you learn your way around the kitchen and our morning routine, it's probably best if I get up."

"Phoebe." He rose and stopped her with a hand on her arm as she moved by him. "I am not trying to take your role in her life away, and I wasn't trying to slam you again for—I just want to learn everything there is to know about her."

She nodded, although she wouldn't look at him. "I'm sorry for getting prickly." The air of tension left and her shoulders sagged. "This is going to take some getting used to."

That it was. He watched as she bent over and picked up a discarded shoe and sock. She'd changed from the neat skirt and blouse she'd worn to school that day into a pair of faded jeans and a T-shirt, although she'd neatly tucked the shirt in and added a belt. Probably her version of hanging-around slob clothes.

Her backside was slim and rounded beneath the jeans. Damn, but he was annoyed with himself. He had a lot more important things than sex to think about tonight, and yet every time he looked at Phoebe all rational thought fled and he became one big walking male hormone.

Bridget let out a squeal and he came back to earth abruptly. Phoebe scooped the baby into her arms. "What are you fussing about, you silly girl?" she asked. "Would you like your daddy to read you a story?"

The kid couldn't exactly answer yes, but Phoebe motioned him over to the big maple rocker and set Bridget in his lap anyway. She came to him as if she'd known him all her short life, settling easily into his lap, then popping her thumb in her mouth. He read the story but after just a few minutes, her little head nodded against his chest and the thumb fell from her slack lips. Glancing down, he realized she'd fallen asleep.

His throat was tight and his chest ached; she was so precious! It was almost too much to believe, that this beautiful child was his.

He wanted to snuggle her against him but he was afraid if he moved she'd wake up. And so he sat with Bridget in his lap until Phoebe stuck her head around the corner of the door frame. "Is she asleep?" she asked in a hushed tone.

He nodded.

She came into the room and knelt at his side, lifting the baby into her arms. As she transferred Bridget's weight, the underside of her breast pressed against his arm for a moment, and her warm, intoxicating, feminine fragrance teased his senses. Instantly, awareness rose, and with it arousal. He wanted to kiss her again. Hell, he wanted to do a lot more than that. He watched silently as she rose to her feet with his child in her arms, and the knowledge that they had made this precious little person together was, oddly, a whole new kind of aphrodisiac. Their daughter had been conceived that day in the hunting cabin, and it didn't take much effort at all to recall the sweet, sizzling passion that had bound them together in far more than just a physical way.

Then Bridget's tiny arms hung limp and her head fell onto Phoebe's shoulder as Phoebe lifted her into her crib. She brushed a kiss across the fiery red curls as she laid the child down, and he swallowed hard, another emotion joining the riot of sensations rushing through him.

How was it possible to go from not even knowing his child existed to loving her more than he loved his own life in less than a day? He didn't even know her, really. And yet…he did. And he would. Another shock jolted him as he realized he could imagine her five years from now—because he'd known her mother at that age as well.

Phoebe turned and left the room on nearly silent feet, and he slowly pushed himself upright. He walked to the crib and gazed down at his daughter for a long moment. *I promise to be the best daddy I can be,* he vowed silently.

Then he followed his child's mother out of the room. They needed to talk about the changes that were about to occur in their lives.

Five

Phoebe was already at the table in her small dining room when he came down the stairs after unpacking his duffel, removing papers from her satchel and making neat piles carefully spaced on the table. She glanced up and sent him an impersonal smile. "Time to grade math tests."

He walked through the living room to her side, looking down at the work she was spreading out before her. "You do this often?"

"Just about every night." She smiled wryly. "The kids complain when I give them assignments, but I really should be the one whining. Every assignment they hand in multiplies my work by twenty-four students." She shrugged her shoulders as she pulled out her chair and took a seat. "It's going to get even more interesting when I start my next class. I'm taking a children's lit class that begins in January."

"I thought you already had a degree."

"Yes." She pulled out an ink pad and a stamp with a smiley face on it. "But in order to keep my teaching certificate I have to do continuing education every so often or work toward my master's degree. The specifics vary from state to state, but the general concept is the same. You probably have to do the same thing—keep your skills current, I mean."

"Yeah. Except now, if I were to stay in the Army, I'd be stuck behind a desk. My ability to hit a target dead center fifty times in a row isn't quite so critical anymore."

She bit her lip and he could see the moment when she realized that she'd reminded him of his forced change of career. Still, she continued to stare up at him, concern in her face. "Will you tell me what happened to you?"

He felt the muscles of his face tightening with the effort to keep a casual expression in place. "I have a piece of shrapnel in my leg. It's too risky to remove." He tried to smile. "Plays hell with airport security."

She didn't return the smile. "I meant how it happened."

He turned away, heading for the living room where he'd laid his book and reading glasses down. "One of my buddies stepped on a mine."

Out of the corner of his eye, he saw her flinch. "Did you see it?"

He nodded. A lump rose into his throat and refused to ease.

"I'm sorry," she said softly.

He managed a nod. "Yeah, me, too."

"You always wanted to be a soldier, didn't you?" A fleeting smile crossed her face. "I remember when Mel and I were about eight, you and the Paylen boys from down the street recruited us to be the enemy."

The lump in his throat dissolved as memory came flooding back, and with it came an irresistible urge to laugh. "Only that didn't last very long once my dad found out we were launching rocks at you out of that homemade catapult." He shook his head ruefully. "He always did have eyes in the back of his head."

Phoebe snorted. "He did not. Melanie ran and told on you."

"That twerp." His tone was fond. "I should have known. She ran and left you there alone. You were picking up the rocks and throwing them back. I never knew a girl could throw that hard, especially one your size."

She smiled smugly. "That's what the other softball players used to say when I was in high school."

Memories of Phoebe as a child, of himself during those same carefree years before the world had demanded its pound of flesh, came flooding back and he returned her grin. "We're lucky, aren't we, to have such good memories? I'd love to go back and be that age again."

To his surprise, her smile vanished. "I don't. You could not offer me anything to live my childhood over again." There was a grim, flat note that he'd never heard before in her voice that told him he'd struck some nerve.

His interest sharpened immediately. "That surprises me," he said.

"Growing up without a father in the picture wasn't always easy."

Now that he thought about it, he could recall occasional unkind comments about the twins' illegitimate birth. But... "You and Mel seemed pretty happy to me."

Her face softened, the line of her mouth relaxing

as her lips curved up the tiniest bit. "We were," she said softly.

He chuckled, determined to get her to relax her guard again. "Happiest when you were tormenting the poor boys in the neighborhood who were all fighting over you."

"You're confusing me with my sister now. I never tormented anybody. All the boys I knew had the hots for Melanie."

"Not all." He said it quietly, but the instant he spoke, the atmosphere changed. Electric awareness sparked and crackled as her gaze flew to his.

But she looked away again immediately. "You, too," she said, and in her face he saw her determination to keep things light between them. "When she and I were seniors, she chased you until you caught her, remember?"

He smiled wryly. "I remember. Are you going to hold it against me forever? I was a teenage boy. And God knows boys that age are helpless against an attractive female who's as determined as Melanie was."

To his surprise, she chuckled. "She *was* determined, too. All she talked about that summer was you. What to wear so that you noticed her, where to stand so that she just happened to be where you were headed. You told her once that she looked

OFFICIAL OPINION POLL

ANSWER 3 QUESTIONS AND WE'LL SEND YOU
2 FREE BOOKS AND A FREE GIFT!

0074823 | FREE GIFT CLAIM # 3953

DETACH AND MAIL CARD TODAY!

YOUR OPINION COUNTS!

Please check TRUE or FALSE below to express your opinion about the following statements:

Q1 Do you believe in "true love"?

"TRUE LOVE HAPPENS ONLY ONCE IN A LIFETIME."
○ TRUE
○ FALSE

Q2 Do you think marriage has any value in today's world?

"YOU CAN BE TOTALLY COMMITTED TO SOMEONE WITHOUT BEING MARRIED."
○ TRUE
○ FALSE

Q3 What kind of books do you enjoy?

"A GREAT NOVEL MUST HAVE A HAPPY ENDING."
○ TRUE
○ FALSE

YES, I have scratched the area below.

Please send me the 2 **FREE BOOKS** and **FREE GIFT** for which I qualify. I understand I am under no obligation to purchase any books, as explained on the back of this card.

326 SDL EFZU

225 SDL EFYK

FIRST NAME

LAST NAME

ADDRESS

APT.#

CITY

STATE/ PROV.

ZIP/POSTAL CODE

www.eHarlequin.com

(STF-D-04/06)

Offer limited to one per household and not valid to current Silhouette Desire® subscribers. All orders subject to approval. Credit or debit balances in a customer's account(s) may be offset by any other outstanding balance owed by or to the customer. Please allow 4 to 6 weeks for delivery.

The Silhouette Reader Service™—Here's How It Works:

Accepting your 2 free books and mystery gift places you under no obligation to buy anything. You may keep the books and gift and return the shipping statement marked "cancel." If you do not cancel, about a month later we'll send you 6 additional books and bill you just $3.80 each in the U.S., or $4.47 each in Canada, plus 25¢ shipping & handling per book and applicable taxes if any.* That's the complete price and – compared to cover prices of $4.50 each in the U.S., and $5.25 each in Canada – it's quite a bargain! You may cancel at any time, but if you choose to continue, every month we'll send you 6 more books which you may either purchase at the discount price or return to us and cancel your subscription.

*Terms and prices subject to change without notice. Sales tax applicable in N.Y. Canadian residents will be charged applicable provincial taxes and GST.

If offer card is missing write to: Silhouette Reader Service, 3010 Walden Ave., P.O. Box 1867, Buffalo NY 14240-1867

BUSINESS REPLY MAIL

FIRST-CLASS MAIL   PERMIT NO. 717-003   BUFFALO, NY

POSTAGE WILL BE PAID BY ADDRESSEE

SILHOUETTE READER SERVICE
3010 WALDEN AVE
PO BOX 1867
BUFFALO NY 14240-9952

NO POSTAGE
NECESSARY
IF MAILED
IN THE
UNITED STATES

good in pink so we shopped for pink for the next three months. Have you ever tried to find a good shade of pink for a redhead to wear?" She shook her head, still smiling. "You didn't stand a chance."

He didn't stand a chance now, either. Did she know how desirable she looked? Her eyes were soft and faraway, her body relaxed where she'd angled herself toward him. Her lips looked so soft and inviting as they curved with happy memories....

They *were* soft and inviting. His entire body revved for action as the memory of the afternoon's kiss leaped into the forefront of his mind again. All he'd wanted to do was sink into her sweetness, live the dream he'd kept in his head during terrifying moments of hiding when he'd been sure he would be discovered any minute. Make love to her for real, not just in his imagination while he lay in an American military hospital in Germany. He'd wanted her so badly he'd nearly forgotten the child playing on the floor mere feet away.

And when he'd remembered, it had taken every ounce of self-control he possessed to look away and focus his attention on his daughter.

"Is it really that bad an idea?"

Her unusually timid tone dragged him out of his introspection. "What?"

She was regarding him with thinly veiled curiosity. "A penny for *those* thoughts. I said you're welcome to invite your father to visit for a few weeks if you like. He might enjoy the chance to get to know Bridget."

"What?" he asked again.

"I said—"

"I know what you said! I guess I'm just…surprised at the offer. Are you sure you want my father underfoot?"

She smiled. "I always liked your father. Unless he becomes a werewolf at the full moon, or has some really weird habits I don't know about, it would be fine with me."

"Or we could take Bridget to California to visit him. He's not a young man anymore, and he's never been on a plane in his life."

A fleeting expression crossed her face so quickly he wasn't even sure if he'd seen it or imagined it. Had it been panic? Dismay? "You could fly home and then come back with him," she said. "You know, so he wouldn't have to fly alone."

"I could." He spoke slowly, watching as she twisted her slender fingers together in a sure sign of nerves. But what the hell was it that was making her so uptight? "Don't you want to come home? See the old neighborhood? You could manage one long weekend, couldn't you?"

Her fingers were practically tied in knots. "I...I guess so." Although, she sounded so reluctant he nearly let it drop. But his curiosity was aroused. She didn't seem to care if she ever went back. Why not? She'd grown up there; her family was buried there. "We can visit Melanie's and your mom's graves, and I can show you where my mother's buried."

"All right." Her voice was quiet. "Let me check the calendar and see when we could go."

Had she really agreed to go back to California with Wade? Phoebe wanted to slap herself silly. He'd been in her life again for just two days and already he was turning her world upside down. She should boot him out.

But she knew she never would. Keeping Bridget's existence a secret had been more than a mistake, it had practically been criminal. And she deserved his anger. She'd really been like that overused cliché—an ostrich with its head in the sand. But at the time, it had been so much easier simply to cut her ties with her old life.

If only she had told his parents about Bridget when she first realized she was pregnant. Or... even after she'd thought he was dead.

But other people would have found out eventually. She could hear them now.

Just like her mother.

At least she knows who the father is. She and her poor sister didn't even have that.

Oh, yes. She knew how small towns could be. At least, the small town where she had grown up. Vicious gossips. Not everyone, of course. She'd known many sweet, wonderful people in her hometown. But she'd known more than she liked of the kind who didn't want to let their daughters come over to play with Phoebe and Melanie.

As if illegitimacy was catching.

If she was thankful for anything, it was for the fact that the world had changed since her own childhood. There were families of every kind out there today, and a child without a father wasn't treated any different than a child with two mothers, or a child who shuttled back and forth between her mother's and father's homes in the middle of the week.

She sighed as she looked at her calendar. She had two days off in October, and if she took off another day, they could go to California for a long weekend and make it back without being so pressed for time that it wasn't even worth the flight. She wasn't sure her courage was up to the task of introducing Wade's father to a grandchild he didn't even know existed, but she could tell that Wade wasn't taking no for an answer.

* * *

"Are you sure you'll be okay? Angie is just one street over if you need her," Phoebe told him for at least the tenth time on Monday morning.

"We'll be fine," Wade said. Again. "I'll call Angie if I need anything. And if anything happens, I'll call you immediately."

"All right. I guess I'll see you this afternoon."

"Bye." He held the door open for her. "Don't worry."

She stopped on the verge of descending the porch steps and looked back at him, a wry expression on her face. "I'm a mother. It's in the job description." Then she heaved a sigh and headed for the car as he closed the front door.

It had taken some fast talking on his part, but yesterday she'd agreed to let him keep Bridget this week without anyone stopping by to check on him. And even better, she'd informed him that she'd worked out her schedule so that they could go to see his dad in just a few weeks. She had to clear it with the principal of her building, but she hadn't anticipated any trouble. So he'd make the plane reservations as soon as she came home and gave him a green light tonight.

His dad. How in hell was he going to explain this to his father? From the time he'd entered adolescence and his dad had sat him down for their first big "talk," the watchwords of the day had been *responsible behavior* and *protection*. Not to mention *morality*.

He'd never mentioned his feelings for Phoebe to his parents, never really had the chance, given what had happened with Melanie's death. And then, after the funeral, after things had gotten so wildly out of control, he hadn't had the chance. He'd had to leave the next morning. And Phoebe hadn't answered her phone, although he'd tried half the night to contact her.

He could have simply walked down the street and banged on her door. Should have, he amended. But he'd known she was grieving, and he'd felt he had to respect that. And he'd felt guilty, taking advantage of her trust when she'd been so vulnerable. He should have stopped her.

In the end, he'd given up, promising himself that he'd get in touch with her in a day or two. But he'd been deployed to Afghanistan earlier than expected, with barely twenty-four hours to prepare and he hadn't had time or opportunity to do anything more than think about her.

A month or two later, he'd learned from his mother that she'd left town, that no one seemed to know where she'd gone. The East Coast, someone thought, so he'd made up his mind to visit her the next time he came home. He'd e-mailed her at the same address he'd used for years now—and to his shock, it was returned as undeliverable. And then his mother had had the stroke and all Wade's phone calls and e-mails with his dad had been filled with medical concerns. He'd only been home twice during that hectic time, once not long after his mom's first stroke, the second after her funeral.

He'd come home for that on a three-day leave and gone right back again afterward. He wouldn't have had time to look up Phoebe if she'd just moved to the next town, much less across the continent. Just days after that, he'd watched one of his buddies die when he'd stepped on an unexpected land mine. Others had been dragged away by insurgents operating out of the Afghanistan mountains. He'd barely been able to conceal himself, but he'd managed it. And then unexpected help in the form of an Afghan villager had saved his life and gotten him back to his own troops. On a stretcher, but alive.

He'd had plenty of time to think about her then, while he'd been recuperating. He'd needed her, had finally admitted to himself that he wanted to see if there was any chance that they might have a future together. He'd considered trying to find her, but he didn't really want to call her and tell her he was lying in a hospital bed. So he'd waited until he was well enough to look for her in person.

But he'd never stopped thinking about her, about any of the all-too-brief time they'd spent together. The revelation of his feelings—and hers, he was pretty sure—at the dance. Which had promptly been put on indefinite hold when Melanie had been killed.

And then Melanie's funeral. Or more specifically, what had occurred right afterward. God, if he'd relived that once he'd been through it a thousand times. And that was probably a conservative estimate. He would never forget making love to Phoebe for the first time, no matter the circumstances....

"Are you okay?"

Phoebe looked up, clearly surprised. She'd been sitting on the swing under the rose trellis at one side of her uncle's home. Just sitting and staring.

Her eyes were red and puffy as she looked at him, and Wade realized what an inane question it was.

"I mean, I know you're not okay, but I didn't want to... I couldn't leave without talking to you."

Her nod seemed to take enormous effort. Slowly, she said, "I just needed a break from it." Her voice trembled. "I can't go back in there and talk about her anymore."

The graveside service was complete; Melanie's family and friends had gathered at her mother's stepbrother's home to console each other, to share memories and simply to visit. It was a terrible thing that it took a funeral to bring everyone in a family together again. Phoebe's father had never been in the family picture, as far as Wade knew. And her mother had passed away the second year the girls were in college. Mrs. Merriman's two stepbrothers lived in the same area, although Wade had never heard either Phoebe or Melanie talk much about their extended family; he'd gotten the distinct impression at the funeral that the family hadn't really approved of Phoebe's mother.

He looked down at Phoebe and a fierce wave of protectiveness swamped him. God, what he wouldn't give to go back to the night of the reunion. He'd almost said no to Mel when she'd asked him to go. If he had, they might not be sitting here today.

But if he hadn't, he might never have realized or appreciated his feelings for Phoebe.

Wade cautiously sat beside her, waiting for her to tell him to get away from her. When he'd first gotten the news about the accident, he'd waited for his doorbell to ring. Waited for Phoebe to come scream at him for sending her twin sister off in such a rage that she'd wrapped her car and herself around a tree as she'd sped away from the reunion.

But Phoebe hadn't come. She hadn't called. And he hadn't dared to contact her. He could hardly move beneath the weight of the guilt he felt; if Phoebe piled more on him, he might just sink right into the ground.

His mother had heard about the funeral arrangements before he had. And it never occurred to her that he might not be welcome. Wade didn't have the heart to explain it all, so he'd gone with his family to the service and tried to stay as far away from Phoebe as he could. God, she must hate him now.

Still, when he'd seen her alone, he'd known he had to talk to her, no matter how she felt about him.

But she didn't seem to hate him. Instead, she leaned her head against his shoulder. "I wish it was last week again." Her tone was forlorn.

"Me, too." She felt as fragile as she sounded. He put an arm around her.

Phoebe sighed and he felt her warm breath through the thin fabric of his dress shirt and t-shirt. "Could we take a walk?"

He nodded. "Sure."

He rose and held out a hand. When she curled her small fingers around his much larger ones, he felt like bursting into song. Entirely inappropriate—and insensitive—under the circumstances.

He led her through the apple orchard and into the forest above the house, following a well-worn path that both wildlife and human had helped to create. They simply walked for a long time. When the path narrowed, he helped her over roots, up steep rises and around boulders, and across a small creek.

They came to a small cabin, a tiny rustic structure. "What's this?" he asked.

"My uncles occasionally use it when they hunt up here."

Along one side was a large pile of wood that looked to him like a grand place for snakes to be hanging out. When Phoebe started forward, he stepped ahead of her, scanning the ground. Most Californians went their entire lives without seeing a rattlesnake; he'd just as soon be one of them.

He pushed open the door of the cabin and stepped inside. When Phoebe followed him, there was barely room for two people to stand in the small space. It held a woodstove, an ax in surprisingly good shape, two wooden chairs and a tabletop that folded flat against the wall, a bunk bed with a mattress nibbled to shreds by squirrels or mice, and two shelves above the table. One shelf was crammed with an assortment of canned goods and a couple packs of matches. The other held a kettle, a large pot and a scant, mismatched pile of dishes with a few spoons and forks thrown in. There was no electricity, no light. An oil lantern and a bucket hung from pegs on the bunks.

"Wow," he said. "I guess this is just for emergencies. But it's got everything you'd need." Indeed, he'd seen much worse in some of the homes in the Afghan villages he'd been through.

"They come up here and clean it out before hunting season each year. They stock it and add a couple of towels and blankets." She rubbed an absent circle in the dust on the table. "We used to play up here. Thought it was the best playhouse in the world."

We, he knew, meant she and Melanie. He imagined to two little girls it had seemed pretty grand. But he didn't know what to say now that she was talking about her twin again, so he didn't say anything.

"One time Mel got her finger pinched pretty badly by a big crawfish we found in the stream," she said, pointing through the open door down the hill to where the pretty little brook wound its way through the dappled shade and rushed over the rough rocks. "And I saw a snake on that rock another day." She smiled a little. "I don't know who scared who more. I screamed. He couldn't move out fast enough."

She stepped back a pace, forcing Wade to move back against the bunks. Even so, her body brushed lightly against his and he was annoyed with his instant reaction. *Relax,* he told himself. *This is not the time to be thinking of sex.*

Phoebe didn't seem to notice that he was getting hard just being close to her. She was looking at the back of the door. When she went still, he put his hands on her hips and moved her a shade to one side so he could see what she'd been looking at.

There, cut into the scarred wood on the old door, were initials. PEM. MAM. Phoebe Elizabeth and Melanie Adeline. He almost smiled thinking about how much Mel had hated that middle name. She'd always complained that Phoebe got the pretty one.

"We did that," she said softly, "when we were about ten. I remember how daring we felt. It was Melanie's idea, of course." She reached out and traced a finger over the rough-hewn initials. "I never told anybody, and I don't think she did, either. It was our big secret." Her voice wavered. "We said we would bring our daughters up here someday and show them."

Her breath began to hitch, and his desire died instantly, submerged beneath concern. He turned her around, and she immediately wrapped her arms around his waist, pressing herself against him like a little animal burrowing into a safe place as she started to sob.

"Hey," he said softly. "Phoebe. Honey." Finally he gave up and just stroked her hair as she cried. His own eyes were a little damp. He'd known and loved Melanie, too. Even though she'd been a brat occasionally, she'd been a part of his life since he was just a kid. She'd been more important than anything else in his life for a short while, until he'd realized that they had very little in common, that he'd never be happy with her. So he'd cut the strings.

He never should have agreed to go to the reunion, but he'd thought it might be fun. Instead, it had been…a revelation. He hadn't anticipated what had happened with Phoebe that night.

How the hell could he have missed it? For so many years, she'd been right next door…and he hadn't seen that the woman of his dreams was right under his nose. No, he'd even dated her sister and still he hadn't realized that Phoebe was the right one for him.

He'd figured it out that night at the dance. Unfortunately, so had Melanie.

Mel hadn't been unkind, he reflected. Just self-absorbed most of the time. She would never have reacted so badly to the sight of Phoebe and him if she hadn't been drunk. He should have realized how out of control she was. But he'd been too wrapped up in Phoebe to care.

And her death was his fault.

Phoebe stirred then, lifting her head. She pressed her mouth to the base of his throat and he felt the moist heat of her breath sear him.

"Hey," he said. A guy could only take so much and he had just reached his limit. He doubted if she even realized how erotic the action had been. He took her arms in a light grasp and tried to step back. "Maybe we should head back."

"I'm in no rush." She spoke against his skin and, this time, she pressed a very deliberate open-mouthed kiss in the same spot. And holy sweet hell, her arms were still around his waist, holding him tight against every soft inch of her.

"Phoebe?" His voice was hushed. "Ah, this isn't such a good idea—"

She kissed the underside of his jaw and then his chin. As she strained upward on her tiptoes, her full weight slid against him. He exhaled sharply. He wasn't going to look down at her. If he did, there was no way he'd be able to keep from kissing her. And if he kissed her, he wasn't going to be able to stop with just a few kisses. Not the way he felt.

He stared straight ahead and set his jaw—

And then she sucked his earlobe into her mouth and her tongue played lightly around it. He dragged in a rough breath of raw desire.

And looked down.

Six

Holy hell.

Wade realized he was still standing at the front door. Which, thankfully, he had already closed, since no one passing by could possibly miss his body's reaction to that memory in the clinging sweatpants he wore. He shook his head ruefully. His system had been at full alert ever since he'd seen Phoebe standing in front of him on her porch Wesnesday afternoon.

It had only been five days ago that he'd found her, he realized with a jolt, and only two since he'd moved in. And yet in some ways it felt very familiar, very comfortable, as if they'd been together a long, long time. Pretty weird considering that they'd never really even dated, much less lived together.

But that was going to change.

He didn't do such a bad job for a novice on his first day alone with Bridget. Phoebe had shown him the whole diapering deal, and had prepared bottles and baby food for lunch. She'd told him that Bridget did well as long as she was kept to a reliable schedule, so he made sure he followed the instructions she'd left for him.

He'd gotten up early with Phoebe and they'd eaten breakfast while she went over the directions she was leaving for him. And then she'd left.

He knew it had been hard for her to walk out the door and leave them alone. If she'd said, "Call me at school if you have any problems," once, she must have said it ten times.

He took Bridget to a park at the end of the street in the morning, then brought her home and gave her a bottle. He didn't even have to rock her, just laid her down in her crib, since her little eyes were practically shut already. Then, while she was sleeping, he opened and dealt with a large envelope of mail that he'd brought with him in case he had time to kill sitting in a hotel room.

Bridget woke up again about two hours later, so he laid a blanket on the living-room floor and played with her there until time for lunch. Phoebe had told him he needed to feed Bridget promptly if he didn't want her to get cranky.

God forbid the kid should get cranky. He'd hate to have to call Phoebe for help. So he heated the mushy-looking stuff Phoebe had left in a small dish and opened up some pureed apricots to mix in with the cereal Phoebe had left out, all of which Bridget devoured as if she hadn't had a square meal in a month. Which he knew was a crock because he'd watched her tuck away a similar mushy mess for breakfast. Not to mention the bottle he'd given her before her nap.

After lunch, he walked around the yard with her in his arms, and they played a little more before she went down for her afternoon nap. When she awakened, he brought her out to the backyard to play until Phoebe got home.

"Hello there!"

Wade glanced away from the sandbox. An elderly woman in a faded brown dress covered by a stained gardening smock stood at the fence between the two yards. She resembled a tiny elf, with white hair twisted up in a messy bun and twinkling eyes that crinkled as she smiled at him.

"Hello." He got to his feet, lifted Bridget from the sandbox and covered the few steps to the fence with his hand outstretched. Before he could elaborate, the elf clasped his hand in a surprisingly firm grip and pumped his arm up and down in vigorous welcome.

"It's so nice to meet you, Mr. Merriman. I'm Velva Bridley, Phoebe's neighbor. She's a dear, dear girl and that little one is too sweet for words." She poked a gnarled finger into Bridget's tummy, eliciting the now-familiar squeal. "Phoebe's never talked much about you. Are you back for good now?"

"Ah, yes. I was in the army in Afghanistan. But yes, I'm here to stay." He figured he'd better get a word in edgewise while he had the chance. Later he could decide whether or not it had been the right word.

"That's wonderful! Just wonderful. Bridget's really at that age now where she needs to have her daddy around. I bet it about killed you to be overseas when she was born. I know it would have done me in for sure, if my Ira had missed an important event like that. Here." She reached into the basket hooked over her arm without even taking a breath and came up with a handful of some kind of pink flowers. "Last snaps of the season. I was going to bring them over after Phoebe got home but you can take 'em in and set 'em in water. Might earn you some points, you know?"

"Snaps?" She'd lost him a few sentences back.

"Snapdragons. I always start mine indoors. Never bring 'em out until the twentieth of May on account of late frosts, my daddy always said, so I start 'em in the house and set 'em out bright and early on the twentieth. Got the first ones in the neighborhood, and the last ones, too," she added proudly. "Mine are hardy."

"That's, ah, that's nice." He cleared his throat. "So you've known Phoebe since she moved in?"

She nodded. "Sweet, sweet girl. I brought her my raisin cake that I always take to new neighbors, and we hit it off right away. I was a teacher a long time ago, before I married my Ira, and my goodness, it's amazing how things have changed in fifty years."

He smiled. "You sound just like my father. He'd happily go back fifty years to what he calls 'the good old days.'"

"Not me!" Velva shook her head. "Give me the age of technology any day. I love being able to instant message my grandchildren and find out what they're up to right that minute."

He almost laughed aloud. As it was, he couldn't

hide his grin. "Computers sure have made communication easier."

"My great nephew is in Iraq," Velva told him, "and getting e-mails a couple times a week really helps his wife to stay strong. I guess you and Phoebe know all about that, though."

"Hello there!"

Wade spun around. Phoebe stood on the back porch of her little house. "Hey," he called back. To Velva, he said, "It was nice to meet you, ma'am. I hope to see you again."

She looked amused. "Well, I expect if you're living next door, you're gonna see me from time to time. Now go greet your wife the way you want to."

Oh, boy. The lady had no idea what she was suggesting. He strode through the yard with Bridget and stepped up onto the back porch. Phoebe stood there in the navy skirt and the matching sweater with crayons on it that she'd worn to work.

"Hi," she said. "How did it—mmph!"

The sentence stopped abruptly as Wade hooked an arm around her waist and brought her up against his free side, setting his mouth on hers at the same moment.

He sought her tongue, sucking lightly and then probing deeply as he felt her body yield to his, her tension evaporating. She had put her hands up and clutched his shoulders when he'd grabbed her, and after a moment she flattened her palms, smoothing them over his back and up to his neck. Kissing Phoebe was like a drug, he decided, juggling the baby so that he could pull her closer. Addictive. Very, very addictive.

When he finally gentled the kiss and released her mouth, he blew out a breath. "Wow."

"What was that for?" She rested her forehead against his shoulder. Her hands slid down his chest and grasped his forearms.

"Ack!" Bridget threw herself forward and Phoebe put up her arms just in time to catch her.

"Hi, sweetie," she said. "We didn't mean to ignore you." Her face was red and she didn't meet Wade's eyes as she jiggled the baby and blew kisses against her neck, making Bridget giggle.

"For Mrs. Bridley," he said.

"Hmm?" She raised her gaze to his, but the connection to her earlier question seemed forgotten.

"The kiss," he said patiently. "Your neighbor is delighted that I'm home from Afghanistan. I didn't think we should disappoint her."

Phoebe's forehead wrinkled. "Oh." It was slightly gratifying to see that his kiss had scrambled her circuits so thoroughly. It was nice to know he wasn't the only one who felt that way.

He reached around her and held the screen door open, ushering her into the kitchen. "Interesting that she thinks you have a husband."

"I never told her that." Phoebe sounded startled.

"I guess she assumed. She's an interesting woman." He gave the adjective special emphasis, and Phoebe finally smiled.

"She's unique."

"Good word for it. How was your day?"

"My—? Oh, fine. How did you two get along?"

"Famously," he assured her. "I managed to change a couple of diapers and get more food into her than on her, and she took both her naps. So I'd say we were successful."

"Good." She looked genuinely pleased. "No emergency calls to Angie, hmm?"

"Nope. Not a one." He took the baby as she got down two glasses and filled them with ice and sweet tea. She cut a slice of lemon, which she squeezed into his, then stirred with a long spoon. As she slid one across the table to where he'd taken a seat, he said, "You remembered."

She stopped with her own glass halfway to her mouth. "Remembered what?"

He lifted his glass as if he were toasting her. "My tea. With lemon."

Her color had almost returned to normal from

their kiss on the porch, but it was back in an instant. "Just a lucky guess," she said.

Right. A warm feeling stole through him. She'd remembered.

She made spaghetti for dinner while he set the table and changed Bridget. It was just bizarre, Wade decided. To go from not even knowing how to find her to living with her in less than a week.

He had anticipated—hoped—that she would still be free and still have feelings for him when he finally tracked her down. And he'd thought about the rest of his life and he'd known he wanted it to include Phoebe. But he'd expected to court her, to date until she felt comfortable with him. So much for expectations, he thought, eyeing the cozy table, the baby in the high chair at one end, and the easy way Phoebe moved around him as if he'd always been there to get in the way.

He'd take this any day, although it certainly hadn't been anything he'd imagined in his wildest dreams.

While they ate, he told her about the other dad with the eight-month-old son he'd met at the park earlier, and she recounted her day. He set Bridget in her infant seat while he helped Phoebe clear the table, and then he said, "I'd like to invite my father to visit at Thanksgiving or Christmas. Do you have a preference?"

She was still looking at him and her eyes went wide. "Thanksgiving or Christmas?" she said faintly. "The holiday season is more than a month away."

He was puzzled. "Yeah. And…?"

"Exactly how long are you planning to stay in my house?" There was a note of what sounded like panic in her voice.

He looked at her closely, unsure he'd heard her right. "I don't have any plans to leave," he said evenly.

"But…but you can't just live with us forever! What if I wanted to—to get married or something?"

"To who?" He couldn't have kept the note of naked aggression out of his voice if he'd tried. He hadn't seen any signs of a man in Phoebe's life, but that didn't mean there wasn't one. "Is there somebody I should be worrying about?"

"No." As soon as the word popped out, she closed her mouth abruptly, as if she was aware that she'd just given him a major tactical advantage.

"Good." He stepped closer and she backed away, but the table was behind her and she couldn't go any farther. And he stepped forward again, until they were almost nose to nose. He reached for her wrists and captured them with his hands, then very slowly leaned forward until their bodies were pressed together from neck to knee. And just like the first time on the dance floor, he felt that little frisson of awareness, that feeling that this was right, click into place. "If you want to get married, that's fine. But the only man who's going to be putting a ring on your finger is me."

She gaped at him. Literally stood there with her mouth hanging open. "Marry…you?" Her voice was faint.

"Yeah." Dammit, she didn't have to act so repelled by the idea.

"No way."

Her instant refusal rattled him, but he wasn't about to let it show. "Why not? We share a child."

"That's not a reason to get married!"

"It is in my book," he said, struggling to keep his voice even. "You and I grew up in the same community, we have a lot of memories in common. We owe it to Bridget to give her a solid foundation." His eyes narrowed. "Don't you ever wish your childhood had been a little different?"

"I—no." She shook her head, avoiding his gaze, and he wished he knew what was going on behind those blue eyes.

"Why not?" he asked again. "Give me three good reasons why you won't marry me."

She was silent, looking aside with her head tilted down.

"You can't, can you?" He still held her hands and he slowly raised them, pulling them around his neck. She didn't embrace him but she didn't drop them when he released her hands and slid his arms around her, settling her more tightly against him. "We are good together, Phoeber," he said in a lower tone, "and you know it as well as I do. We know each other so well. We could make this work."

He put one hand beneath her chin and lifted her face to his, slowly setting his lips on hers. Her mouth was warm, her lips pliant as he kissed her, but slowly she began to respond, kissing him back with an ever-growing fervor that he remembered from the single time he'd made love to her. The response awakened the need for her that always lurked just beneath the surface, and he growled deep in his throat as he gathered her even more closely against him, pressing her head back against his shoulder as he sought the depths of her mouth.

She clung to him, giving him everything he demanded. Sliding one hand up her hip, he slipped it beneath the bottom of her sweater. The skin above the waistband of her skirt was warm and silky, and an even stronger surge of desire shook him.

"Marry me," he muttered against her mouth.

"This isn't fair," she said, pulling her mouth back far enough to get the words out.

He kissed the line of her jaw. "I don't care about fair. All I care about is making us a family."

Was it his imagination or did her body tense the slightest bit?

It was definitely not his imagination that she withdrew from the kiss slowly but surely, stepping back and straightening her sweater. "Give me time to think about it. This is the rest of my life we're talking about here." Her voice was quiet but he recognized that tone. When Phoebe dug in her heels about something, there was no budging her short of using dynamite. And he had the sneaking suspicion that might not even do it.

"It's the rest of all of our lives," he reminded her.

"I know." She sounded weary. "Let me think about it."

"When can I expect an answer?"

She spread her hands. "I don't know. We can talk again…when we come back from California. All right?"

He nodded grudgingly, not happy about it but unwilling to push further in case he really annoyed her and she decided she couldn't stand him for the rest of her life. "All right."

The following weekend, Wade made the travel arrangements for their California trip. The weekend after that, they left right after Phoebe took leave from school at lunch on Friday.

Bridget fussed for a bit early in the flight but, after a bottle and some cuddling, she settled down and went to sleep for a while. As Phoebe looked down at the beautiful baby girl in her arms, she was amused again by the determined little chin…oh, that was Wade all over.

Wade. Amusement faded as she thought of his marriage proposal, if it could even have been called that, and the fist squeezing her heart tightened painfully. He wanted to marry her to make a home for their child, and because they knew each other well enough to make it work. But he hadn't said anything about love.

Could she marry him, knowing that he didn't love her the way she wanted? Oh, he cared for her, she didn't doubt that. And he clearly desired her. But he'd *loved* and desired Melanie once, and she knew that her sister would always hold his heart. She, Phoebe, had never expected that she'd have any part of him, much less marry him and bear his children, so how could she complain?

As the jet began its landing descent, Phoebe hungrily gazed out the window. There was Mission Bay, the water sparkling in the sunlight, and the golf course of La Jolla. The university, the naval base, the zoo. The lighthouse, high atop a cliff.

The freeway heading north was packed with traffic all rushing to exit the city, all driving at typical breakneck speed California-style. She could hardly wait to be in the middle of it.

And before she knew it, they were. Wade had rented a car for the long weekend since he didn't have a car of his own. He'd never seen the need before, he'd told her. When he'd come home, he'd just driven one of his parents' vehicles.

As they entered the outskirts of their old neighborhood, Phoebe realized she was holding her breath.

It still looked much the same. Small yards shaded by flowering trees; tricycles, bikes and skateboards littering yards and driveways; brilliantly colored flowers fronting many of the carefully kept small homes.

You could see the ocean from the end of their block, she knew. And as Wade drove to the end of the dead-end street and turned around so that he could stop the car along the curb in front of his father's house, she craned her neck to look out over the steep cliff just beyond the barrier the city had placed there.

She couldn't see the beach, which had to be

reached by going down a steep, winding road from the top of the hill, but the vast expanse of the ocean lay before her. Today it was a deep, dark blue, with bouncing whitecaps tossing spray into the air in all directions. A wave of nostalgia hit her like a rough breaker, smashing over her, swamping her.

She'd missed that view so much. Who was she kidding? She wasn't an East Coast girl. She loved the wild, untamed Pacific. She wanted Bridget to grow up with memories of smooth, rounded cobblestones littering the beach, of water so cold it made your teeth chatter. She wanted to take her daughter to the pretty beach in Laguna Niguel where they had spent a day each year on a sort of family mini-vacation, to tell her stories about her grandmother and her Aunt Melanie….

But it was harder here, Phoebe thought, swallowing. Here where all the memories of her sister and her mother lurked, it was harder to ignore her grief and go on. That had been one of the main attractions about the job in New York. But now the past she'd run from had caught up with her, and because of her own stupidity, she owed it to Wade to stop running and let him get to know his daughter.

Phoebe turned her gaze to her old home, four doors down the street, wondering about the family who lived there now. Did they have a pet? Her mother's poodle, Boo-Boo, had dug holes all over their backyard until he'd gotten too old to do more than lie on the porch and yap at the neighborhood kids on their bikes.

Were there children? She couldn't tell from the outside. The garage door was down and there were no bikes or kid equipment littering the yard. And a tall hedge made it impossible to see into the backyard. Was the lemon tree her mother had planted still there?

"Hey." Wade's voice was quiet. "You okay?" He touched her back lightly.

"I'm okay." She squared her shoulders. "It's odd to come back here and not be able to go home, if you know what I mean."

He nodded. "I can imagine, even though I've never experienced it."

But in a way, he had. "How different is it without your mom?"

He shrugged. "Not so. Dad always did give her a hand with the housework and cooking, so it's not like he was helpless."

"But the dynamics change." Oh, did they ever. Some of the most miserable times of her life had been the weekends and college breaks she'd spent at home in the first year after her mother had passed away. It wasn't like it had once been before between Melanie and her. They'd each been grieving, but instead of drawing closer, their grief had isolated them and she'd found herself reluctant to visit as much. It was easier to stay on campus and immerse herself in her life there than it was to go home and enter the silent world of grief that she and Melanie had shared. Mel had stayed in their house, gone to a community college. She'd never really gotten away from the memories and Phoebe had sometimes wondered if Mel resented her for that. It had been Melanie's choice to keep living there, but had it kept her grief from lightening?

Phoebe grieved, too, but life had gone on and, somewhere along the way, she'd made the decision to do the same thing.

"I guess you know all about the way a family changes," he said quietly.

She nodded.

"When your mom died, things changed. But after Melanie died, your whole world was different, wasn't it?" The quiet sympathy in his voice was nearly her undoing.

She swallowed. "Yes. Losing Mom was hard. But losing Mel… Logically, I know that her death wasn't the catalyst for my life taking such an unexpected turn, but sometimes it seems as if one thing just led to the next."

A muscle jumped in his jaw and she realized he had clamped his teeth tightly together. "I guess it must." He sounded as if his words were being dragged from him and she glanced at him, wondering what on earth was wrong.

"Are you feeling well?" she asked as she unbuckled Bridget's car seat.

That appeared to startle him. "Yeah." He indicated the child still sleeping on her mother's shoulder. "Let's go in and introduce Sleeping Beauty here to her grandpa."

Phoebe's stomach was in knots as Wade guided her to the side porch door that the family always used. He opened the door and gestured for her to precede him. As he entered behind her, he called, "Hey, Dad. Where are you?"

"Hello." A deep rumbling voice much like Wade's came from the direction of the kitchen.

Wade stepped around her and headed down the hallway leading to the kitchen, and a moment later his father appeared. "Well, this is a surprise! I thought you were going to be on the East Coast for at least a month." The two men grabbed each other in a typically male, back-pounding hug.

Phoebe stood, rooted to the spot in horror. A *surprise?* Hadn't Wade told his father about Bridget yet?

"...someone here I want you to meet," Wade was saying as the men walked toward her.

Reston, Wade's father, did a double take when he saw her standing there. "Phoebe Merriman. I didn't know you were back in town, honey! It's great to see you—and who's this?" His tone was filled with delight. "I didn't even know you'd gotten married and here you're a mama."

An immediate silence fell, awkwardness hanging in the air like thick smoke.

"Aw, hell." Reston scrubbed a hand over his face. "Forget I just said that. Mothers don't have to be married these days, I know." He stumped on toward Phoebe, and she remembered that his uneven gait was the result of arthritis that forced him to favor one hip. When he reached her, he peered down at the sleeping child she had shifted to hold in the cradle of her arm. "Aren't you a beauty?" he asked, his tone tender as he brushed a finger along Bridget's cheek, catching one fiery curl on his fingertip. He chuckled. "Got that Merriman red hair, didn't she?"

Phoebe nodded, forced herself to smile. "When she was born, all the nurses laughed because it was sticking straight out all over her head."

Wade cleared his throat. "Ah, Dad? Can we sit down?"

Reston straightened and shot his son a wary look. "Okay. You bringing bad news?"

Wade shook his head. "No, I think you're going to like this news." He ushered Phoebe ahead of him into the living room and took a seat beside her on the couch. "There's no easy way to tell you this, so I might as well just say it. Phoebe and I…well, the baby's name is Bridget and I'm her father."

Seven

I'm her father.

Phoebe wondered if Wade's words sounded as shocking to his parent as they did to her. How long was it going to take before she accepted that Wade was really alive—and in her life for good, if he had his way?

Reston Donnelly's eyes widened and his mouth fell open. "Get out!"

"It's true." Wade smiled at his father's obvious astonishment. "You're a grandfather."

Reston's gaze flew back to Bridget. "That's—you're—she's my granddaughter?"

Wade nodded.

"Why…?" Reston cleared his throat. "Why didn't you tell me?"

"He didn't know," Phoebe said hastily. She couldn't bear the look of hurt on Reston's face. "I'm sorry I didn't tell you—"

"Phoebe thought I was dead." Wade cut off her attempt at apology. "She heard the first news after my unit got cut off, but she never got the correction when I was found."

Reston's head snapped up from his inspection of Bridget, his expression changing from hurt to horrified. "Oh, honey. If I'd known where to find you, I'd have let you know. No one knew where you'd gone after…"

"I know. I needed a fresh start."

Reston nodded. He looked back down at the child in Phoebe's arms. "I imagine you did." His gaze landed on his son. "How'd you find her?"

Wade uttered a short bark of laughter. "Hounded every person she'd ever known, hoping someone could tell me where she was. I finally got lucky with one of her high-school friends."

"Must have been the shock of your life when he showed up alive." Reston transferred his gaze back to Phoebe.

"You could say that." No way was she getting into that minefield. "Would you like to hold her?"

Reston nodded. "You bet." Phoebe's heart melted at the look in Wade's father's eyes. Dazed. Delighted. Tender.

Reston nodded. "Please." He settled back in his chair as Phoebe rose and approached, laying Bridget in his arms. He cradled her in one gnarled hand, gently brushing her cheek with the other. "Oh, you're a little beauty," he whispered. "Bridget. Bridget Donnelly. That's a good Irish name." He shook his head and the light reflected the sheen of tears in his eyes. "Your grandma surely would have loved you."

Phoebe's chest hurt as she fought not to sob. She didn't dare glance at Wade. She could imagine the wintry expression on his face without having to see it. But she didn't try to correct Reston's assumption about Bridget's last name. There would be time for that.

Bridget started to fuss and Wade said, "Here. Let me see if I can settle her." Phoebe did glance at him then, but he wasn't looking at her. He lifted the baby and held her against his shoulder; it was amazing how natural the gesture looked after such a short time. Bridget quieted immediately and Wade grinned. "She's turning into a daddy's girl."

Phoebe relaxed, one of those silly maternal things that happened when one's child was well-behaved. Before Bridget, she'd never understood how parents could be so uptight. A screaming session in the middle of Wal-Mart could change your perspective pretty quickly. She dug in her bag and handed Reston a photo album into which she had slid pictures of Bridget right after her birth and at various ages since. "I brought you some pictures."

Reston moved to the sofa and patted the seat beside him. His face was soft. "Sit down here and tell me about her."

"I'll join you." Wade's voice was quiet.

She glanced up at him, but he was looking at the album and wouldn't meet her gaze. She knew he'd looked through the photo albums she'd kept since Bridget's birth…but she'd never told him much about his daughter's early days, she realized.

Remorse shot through her for about the zillionth time, and she mimicked his father's motion, patting the cushion on the other side of her. "That would be nice. I haven't told you that Bridget was almost born in the middle of a wedding."

Wade froze. "What?"

She tugged on his arm and he sank down beside her, patting Bridget's back in a distracted manner.

Smiling, she opened the photo album. On the first page, she'd placed the only picture she had of herself during her pregnancy.

"This picture was taken the day Bridget was born. I went to the wedding of a coworker and the photographer snapped this shot before the service while I was standing at the guest book." She chuckled. "It's a good thing he got a picture of me then!"

"You went into labor at the wedding?" Wade was looking a little green around the edges.

"I was already in labor," she corrected. "But I was too dumb to realize it until about halfway through the ceremony. I just thought my back hurt from being on my feet so much the day before."

Reston guffawed. "Bet you'll never be that dumb again."

A silence followed his hoot of laughter. A *pregnant* silence, she thought, as she cast around for a response. Would she ever be pregnant again?

Wade wanted her to marry him…but she hadn't really let herself dwell on exactly what that would mean. Would he want other children?

An involuntary quiver deep in her belly made her shiver suddenly as her thoughts immediately turned to how those children would be created. Every nerve cell in her body homed in on Wade's large, warm body sitting so close to hers. Hastily, she shoved the photo album into Wade's hands and leaped to her feet. "I'd like to freshen up."

Sometimes it seems as if one thing just led to the next.

Wade could still hear the grief in Phoebe's voice as he lay in the single bed in his childhood room that night. That phrase had been haunting him.

God, but he felt like the lowest of the low. She hadn't said it, and he was pretty sure she hadn't even thought about how it had sounded. But he knew that her life would never have turned out the way it had if it wasn't for him.

If it wasn't for you getting her pregnant, you mean.

Well, yeah, that was what he'd meant. If he'd kept his hands off her, if he'd given her the comfort that she'd really needed instead of the sex she'd thought would make her forget the pain, if he'd been less of a self-absorbed jerk afterward…. If, if, if.

No point in going any farther down that road. It was what it was. He and Phoebe had a daughter together. And they owed it to Bridget to work out their issues and give her the happy, stable home she deserved.

Which was why he had to figure out a way to get Phoebe to marry him. She had seemed so resistant to the idea. Why?

He was sure it wasn't physical. God knew, they had enough chemistry between them to start a brush fire.

Unable to sleep, he rose and padded down the stairs in his bare feet. The little photo album Phoebe had given his father lay on the coffee table in the living room. The streetlight outside cast a few bars of light across the room and he idly picked up the scrapbook and flipped through it. Phoebe had spent more time earlier taking them through Bridget's young life. Rolling over, sitting up, first teeth. Stuff he would have laughed at if the married guys in his unit had talked about it.

"Wade?"

Startled, he nearly dropped the album and he juggled it for a moment until he had it in his hands again. Phoebe stood on the lowest step.

"What are you doing?"

Her hair was down. Even in the darkened room, he could tell it was long. Longer than it had been a year and a half ago. He hadn't realized it because, until now, she'd worn it scrambled up in a messy knot atop her head. It should have looked ridiculous but it was oddly charming. And even more so since he was pretty sure she hadn't tried for that effect. For Phoebe, it was expedient to shove her hair up out of the way.

If it had been Melanie, she'd probably have worked on it for an hour in front of a mirror to achieve a like effect. *Melanie.* Were they ever going to talk about her? Her memory hovered between them like a helium balloon tied to a kid's hand.

"Are you all right?" She was standing there with a concerned look on her face, clad in what resembled a men's-style button-down shirt, although from the way it caught her at mid-thigh and fit her curves, he was pretty sure it hadn't been designed for a man.

"I'm not sure," he said slowly.

Before he knew what she intended, she was down the steps and across the room, placing one small, cool hand on his brow. "Do you feel sick?"

He looked at her, standing so close to him in the shadows of the small living room, her eyes wide and worried. "No," he said. "I'm not sick."

Immediately she began to withdraw her hand but he caught it before she could move away. "Don't go."

She stilled, but didn't speak. Her gaze flew to his face again as he tugged on her hand, drawing her closer. He threaded one hand through her hair, cupping her cheek, and rubbed his thumb lightly over her lips. She swallowed. "Wade, I…" She stopped and shook her head. "I'm glad we came to visit your father."

He smiled, letting his hand drift from her face to play with the cool, silky strands of hair. "Me, too. Bridget's already got him wrapped around one of those little fingers. Thanks for letting him give her a bottle tonight."

"He never stopped talking to her the entire time. Did you notice that?"

He nodded. "He sounded pretty ridiculous."

"Like someone else I know."

"Hey! I do not sound ridiculous."

"You're right," she agreed. "Just infatuated. Totally, ridiculously infatuated."

"It would be impossible not to be," he agreed. "She's perfect."

"Well, almost, maybe," she conceded.

"She's a lot like her mother," he said. "Wrapping men around her little finger."

She snorted beneath her breath. "You know darn well I never wrapped a man around any part of me."

Silence fell between them as her retort registered.

Immediately, his thoughts turned to the cabin in the woods where he'd made love to her. She'd been wrapped around him then, her long, slim legs gripping his hips as he'd plunged into her with so little restraint he winced at the memory even as his body responded to it. "I'd have to disagree with that," he said, aware that his voice had roughened.

Phoebe moaned softly, dropping her head so that her hair fell forward to hide her expression. "Bad choice of words."

He put a finger beneath her chin. She might not be willing to talk about Melanie, but he'd be damned if he was going to let her ignore what was between them, too. "Not so bad. It reminds me of making love with you." He caressed her bottom lip with his thumb again. "Do you remember what it was like between us?"

She drew her breath in sharply and her body tensed. For a moment, he thought she wasn't going to answer him at all. But finally, she whispered, "I remember."

He was more pleased than the two small words warranted that she'd admitted it. Sliding his arms around her, he drew her close. "Let's make a new memory."

She didn't resist as he found her mouth with his. His pulse doubled its rate when he felt her small hands creep around his back. Her mouth was soft and yielding beneath his, her body equally so. Touching the closed line of her lips with his tongue, he gently traced the tender seam until she opened for him, then deepened the kiss as he gathered her closer.

He took her arms and pulled them up around his neck as he feasted on her mouth. She was so much shorter than he was that she had to stand practically on her toes, throwing her off balance and bringing her body to rest against his. Her soft belly pressed against him and his hardening shaft nestled into the cleft at her thighs, sending a surge of pleasure dancing up his spine.

Tearing his mouth from hers, he kissed a trail along the silken column of her neck, then nuzzled the collar of the nightshirt out of the way. She had only buttoned it as high as the one between her breasts, and he exposed a generous expanse of her pale flesh until the shirt drooped off one shoulder.

"Beautiful," he breathed against her skin. He brought up a hand and cupped one breast in his palm, lightly brushing his thumb across the nipple through the thin fabric of the shirt.

She made a small sound and her head fell back.

"The baby was fussing so I—" Reston stopped halfway down the stairs with Bridget in his arms. Even in the dim light, Wade could see his father's eyebrows rising.

Phoebe jerked upright with a startled sound, but when she tried to pull away, Wade refused to let her go. She buried her face in the front of his shirt as Wade met his father's speculative gaze over her head.

"You do know this is how you got the first one, right?"

Wade couldn't prevent the snort of laughter that escaped. "No, Dad," he said. "This is absolutely, positively *not* it."

It was Reston's turn to grin while Phoebe made a quiet moan of mortification. "So," he said. "You gettin' married?"

"Yes," said Wade.

"No," said Phoebe.

If his father's eyebrows had moved any higher they'd have merged with his hairline. "I see." He turned and started back up the stairs with the baby, who appeared to have gone back to sleep. But just before he disappeared, he stopped and looked back, and his shadowed eyes held a sober expression that contrasted sharply with the grin of a moment ago. "That would please your mother," he said quietly to Wade. Then he looked at Phoebe, who still hadn't moved. He shook his head and his shoulders slumped. "Sometimes I still can't believe she's not here. She'd be tickled down to her toes with that baby girl."

"Old manipulator," Wade said quietly when he was sure his father was out of earshot.

Phoebe lifted her head from Wade's chest, although she couldn't bring herself to meet his eyes. His father's final words echoed in her ears, awakening all the guilt and remorse she felt for keeping the news of Wade's child to herself.

Looking down the path her life was about to follow, it didn't take a fortune-teller to predict heartbreak. Then again, if she didn't marry him, that was a given.

She knew she was going to say yes, even before she opened her mouth. She'd rather live with Wade, knowing he didn't love her the way she craved, than live without him. She'd thought he was dead and gone forever and it had felt as if half of her had died, too. She was going to take him any way she could get him, regardless of the pain she knew lay in wait.

"All right," she said quietly.

"What?" Wade looked puzzled. He was still staring at the doorway where his father had been a moment ago.

"All right, I'll marry you."

That got his attention. Wade's gaze shot to hers again and his gray eyes focused on her with a blazing intensity that made her cringe inwardly. "My father catching us kissing made you change your mind?"

She shrugged. "I just—I know Bridget deserves a family. An intact family," she amended. He'd been right. A child *was* a good reason to get married. Every child deserved a set of parents.

*And grandparents. I will never forgive myself
for depriving her of knowing her paternal grandmother. If it was for a day, or a month, or even
years and years, I should have thought about how
they would feel.*

Wade was looking down at her and his eyes still
felt like two lasers examining her soul.

God, had she really just agreed to marry this
man? This man whom she'd loved since she'd been
a child on the playground? She had reasons, she
reminded herself. Bridget needed a father; she
deserved a stable childhood with two parents.
Raising a family on a teacher's salary could be
done, but it wouldn't be easy. With Wade's help,
they'd be able to give their daughter the things
Phoebe wanted for her: music or dance lessons,
sports opportunities, all the myriad activities that
children of the modern world pursued.

Phoebe, on the other hand, only needed one
reason to marry Wade: love. She'd loved him for
what seemed like forever. And then he'd died and
she'd had to accept it, though it had felt as if her
heart had been permanently shattered.

And then…then she'd found out he hadn't
died at all.

Her stupid heart had bounced back a lot faster
than her head. She was still having trouble believ-

ing that all this was real. But her heart was having no trouble at all loving Wade with even more intensity than she had when she was seventeen years old and he'd belonged to her sister.

"Good," Wade finally said, startling Phoebe out of whatever internal argument she was having with herself. The expressions fleeting across her face ranged from tenderness to the deepest sadness he'd ever seen. He wasn't sure he wanted to know what she was thinking about. "When?"

"I don't know!" She looked startled again. "Do we have to decide tonight?"

He nodded. "Yeah. Before you change your mind." He snapped his finger. "I know. We could stop in Vegas on the way home."

Phoebe's expression was horrified; he almost laughed out loud. "I am *not* getting married in a quickie wedding chapel in the gambling capital of the world! Besides, what would we do with Bridget?"

He shrugged. "Take her with us?"

"No," she said. "Absolutely, positively no way. We go back to New York and apply for a license like normal people, wait until we get it, and do this right. I have no intention of telling Bridget we got married in Las Vegas on the spur of the moment."

"Or our other children." He tried to make it sound innocent; he couldn't resist teasing her.

"Our other—" She stopped and narrowed her eyes. "You said that just to rattle me," she accused.

He grinned. "Did it work?"

A wry smile lifted the corners of her mouth. "I guess it did."

He was still embracing her, still deeply aware of the pounding of his pulse, of her soft curves and the way her hips cradled him. Holding her gaze, he put both hands on her hips and pulled her more firmly against him. Then he shifted his hips slightly, pressing himself so snugly against her that he nearly groaned aloud. "I want you," he said quietly.

She closed her eyes. "Not here." Her voice was so soft he could barely hear her.

"No." He pressed a short, hard kiss to her full pink lips. "Not here. But soon."

Eight

They were off the plane in New York and heading away from the airport. Bridget had just fallen asleep in her car seat when Wade said, "Thank you for letting me bring Bridget out to meet Dad. He adored her."

He glanced over to see Phoebe smiling a little uncertainly. "You don't have to thank me." The smile faded. "I should have gotten in touch with you as soon as I found out I was pregnant."

Unspoken between them was the knowledge that his mother had never known she had a grandchild on the way, or a granddaughter.

"You should have," he agreed.

Even from the driver's side, not looking right at her, he could tell that Phoebe's body went stiff. The temperature in the car dropped about ten degrees. If he'd been looking to pick a fight, he'd have been satisfied with the first volley. But...

"But I understand why you didn't. And maybe it wouldn't have mattered," he said, and with the words, the hard knot of anger that had hidden deep inside him finally uncoiled. "My mother's body was giving out. After she had the first stroke, I learned a lot more about strokes, what causes them, what kind of progress stroke patients make, what therapies are used.... It's probably a blessing for both her and my dad that she didn't live for years with minimal function."

"How can you say that? Don't you think your dad would rather have had her alive in any condition—"

"I'm sure he thinks he would have. But while I was recuperating I saw a lot of victims of head injury and soldiers who'd had strokes after other catastrophic injuries. And I know my mother never would have wanted to live like that." He paused. "There's no dignity in some kinds of living. I wouldn't have liked that for either of them."

She nodded and her silky hair slid over the back

of his hand. It felt like cool silk and his one-track mind instantly shot ahead to the night looming before them. The night when they would put Bridget to bed and then it would just be the two of them. Alone.

The next few hours crawled by. They arrived back at Phoebe's house and unpacked the car, then had a late dinner. They'd lost three hours on the trip east but it was still only eight o'clock when Bridget went down for the night.

Wade followed Phoebe into the room as she laid the baby in her crib, and they looked down at her together.

"She's incredible," he said softly.

Phoebe smiled. "She is, isn't she?"

He put his arm around her shoulders and led her from the room. Phoebe tugged the door nearly shut as they entered the hallway. When she turned back to him, she met his eyes with a wry smile and blew out a breath. "I'm nervous," she said with a laugh.

He smiled. "You don't have to be." He took her hand and led her into the bedroom and across to the big bed in which she slept. Setting his hands on her shoulders, he drew her to him and slid his arms around her, simply holding her, absorbing the amazing sensation of having Phoebe in his arms.

She slipped her arms around his waist and snuggled close.

It was a sweet, sweet moment. Wade felt his heart swell with emotion. *I love you.*

He nearly said it aloud. Might have, except that he was a coward. Plain and simple, a coward.

The night they'd danced, he thought Phoebe had indicated she could care for him. But was it long-term? Sure, she'd made love with him—after her sister's funeral when no one in their right mind could say her judgment was sound. And she'd clearly been overwhelmed to see him again after she'd thought he was dead. But he was the father of her child. And they'd been friends since their own childhood. She didn't have to love him to be thrilled that he was alive.

She got so quiet every time Melanie's name came up that he could barely stand it. Did she blame him? God knew, she wouldn't be wrong. He should never have let Mel leave alone that night.

So he didn't speak aloud. Her very silence suggested that her heart wasn't entirely in this relationship and that made him nervous as hell. She might never forgive him for Melanie's death but there was no way he was going to let her shove him out of her life. He loved her, even if he could never tell her.

Tonight, he would show her.

He stopped beside the bed and took her into his arms. After a moment, she lifted her face to him and his heart leaped as he lowered his mouth to hers. Whatever else was between them, there was no arguing with the chemistry they created together. He kissed her for a long, long time, using his lips and tongue to show her how he felt, simply made love to her mouth until they both were breathing hard and his blood was pounding through his veins.

When he lifted the hem of her T-shirt, she raised her arms and let him pull it over her head. She shook her head as he tossed the shirt aside and her hair fell around her shoulders, emphasizing the lacy white bra she wore.

"You're beautiful." He reached around her and dispensed with the bra, and wanted to howl at the moon when the full, firm mounds of her breasts, capped by rosy nipples, were revealed. He cupped them in his hands and smoothed his thumbs over the taut tips as she lifted her hands to the buttons of his shirt.

She managed to get about half the buttons undone before she threw her head back with a half laugh and said, "I can't concentrate."

He smiled, lowering his head to the slope of her breast and tasting the tender flesh. "Can I help?"

He quickly tore the shirt open and shrugged it off, then unfastened his pants as well and pushed them off along with his boxers. Turning his attention to her pants, he unzipped them and put his thumbs at the sides, pushing until she, too, had kicked the last of her clothing away.

Then he urged her onto the mattress.

As he followed her down, he said, "Do you have any idea how many times I dreamed about this?" He cupped her breast again, pulling her close with one arm beneath her head. "You kept me warm on a lot of damn cold nights halfway around the world."

To his shock, her eyes filled with tears. "I was so mad at you for leaving," she said. "For not coming to say goodbye. And then—and then—"

And then she'd thought he was dead. Gone forever. He read the anguish in her eyes.

"Shh," he said. "I'm here, and I'm never leaving again." He smoothed a hand down over the silky skin of her belly as he bent his head and took one nipple into his mouth. Suckling strongly, his own body pulsed in response as her back arched off the bed and her hands threaded through his hair to hold him to her.

He eased his weight over her, settling himself into the heated cove between her thighs, feeling the damp curls and the soft, soft flesh below. He couldn't wait.

Slowly, he pushed into her, groaning at the tight, slick feel of her body clasping his. Too tight, he realized belatedly.

"Relax, baby, you're okay." He stopped moving and held every muscle still, though his body was screaming at him to move. Guilt ate at him. He should have been thinking of her, and instead all he'd been able to do was think about how badly he wanted to be inside her. It wasn't even completely sexual, but something more, instinct urging him to stamp every inch of her with his scent and feel, to make her his again in the most basic way there was.

"I'm sorry," she whispered, squirming with discomfort. "I had a couple of stitches after Bridget was born and—"

"Shh," he said, kissing away a tear that trailed from the corner of her eye. "It'll be okay. We're in no hurry here."

She was taking deep, fast breaths, her breasts heaving as she fought to cooperate, and he knew he needed to help her. He didn't want her first time after Bridget's birth to be something she just wanted to forget.

He lifted himself a little away from her and stroked one hand between them, down her belly to the spot where they were joined. His fingers found the tiny, tender button hidden in her curls. Lightly, hoping that she would enjoy his touch, he rubbed a finger over her. And nearly had a heart attack when her body jolted involuntarily beneath his, driving him even deeper into her tight sheath.

She sucked in a sharp breath and he said, "Did you like that?"

He felt, more than saw, her nod in the darkness, so he did it again, starting a small circular pattern that massaged the little nubbin gently. Her hips began to move beneath his and he felt her muscles quiver. His own muscles were trembling with the effort it took to hold still when everything within him was urging him to thrust forward, but still he resisted. Her hips were moving steadily now, creating a delicious rhythm in time with his circling finger and he locked his jaw, holding on to his control by the slimmest of threads as her motions drew him in and out, in and out.

"Oh, yeah," he said through clenched teeth, "Oh, baby, I'm sorry—I can't—I can't—"

Wait was what he'd meant to say, but he never got the chance. Without warning, she arched beneath him and he felt an incredible sensation as she came in heavy waves of completion, her inner muscles squeezing his aching flesh over and over again. Control fell away and he shoved his hips forward, then withdrew and hammered into her again.

She was still shaking and jerking beneath him as he felt his body gather, gather, gather—and then release in a hot, drenching burst of pleasure that went on and on and on until both of them lay spent, gasping for breath.

His head was on the pillow beside hers and he smiled as she turned her head and pressed her lips briefly to his.

The sweetness of the gesture humbled him. How had he left this woman without telling her that he intended to return and make her his forever? He'd been so wrapped up worrying about what he'd done to her when she was grieving and vulnerable, so determined to give her space to think, that he'd nearly lost his opportunity forever.

What if she'd met and married someone after she'd thought he'd been killed? The idea didn't bear thinking about.

Instead, he focused on the one thing that had been nagging at him since their discussion over the weekend. "So when do you want to get married?" he asked.

He felt her smile against his throat. "Sounds like you already have a time in mind."

"Yeah." He snorted. "Yesterday. How long will it take to get a license here in New York, anyway?"

"I have no idea what the law is here," she said. "Since you'll be home this week, why don't you find out? I assume that once we have a license we can just go to the courthouse."

"All right. Is that what you want?" he asked. "A civil ceremony?"

She shrugged and the motion sent a pleasurable chain reaction rippling through his system. "I don't need a big church wedding, if that's what you're asking. It would seem sacrilegious, given that we already have a child." She stopped, then said, "Unless you think that would be important to your dad. Will you invite him?"

He was warmed by the concern she showed for his father's feelings. "I'll invite him, but I doubt Dad is about to get on a plane. Not even for that. He's not going to care if we get married here."

"All right." She nodded, as if that were settled. "You find out what we need to do and we'll set a date."

He nodded. "Leave it to me." Then he moved his hips experimentally and grinned when her body clenched around him. "Hmm, wonder what we can do until then?"

She laughed as she drew his head down to hers.

And as he began to kiss her again, he thought of an idea for a unique wedding gift that he knew would mean a great deal to her. It was time to lay some ghosts to rest.

But he could pursue that tomorrow. Right now, he had better things to do.

A week passed, then two. They decided to get married in the first week of December, a simple ceremony at the county courthouse, and Phoebe planned ahead to take a personal day.

One evening in the beginning of November, he said, "I applied for a job in the private sector today. The thought of being stuck behind a desk working for the Department of the Army, having to move every couple of years, doesn't appeal to me."

She looked up from the papers she was grading. "What kind of work is it?"

He lifted a glossy dark folder that he'd been reading and passed it to her. "Private security."

"As in being a bodyguard?" She tried not to let her dismay show. Wouldn't a bodyguard need to live with or near his employer? Possibly travel with the individual, as well?

"Not exactly." He smiled. "I heard about this company from a friend of mine who got out of the service and went to work for them. This firm performs a number of different specialized services. They are called in when kidnappings occur, they're quietly hired for operations that the government wants done without any fanfare, they set up protective services for people and property. Last year they provided security for a huge gem exhibit at the Met."

"What's it called and where is it?"

"Protective Services, Inc." He hesitated. "The main company is located in northern Virginia, but they're planning on starting up at least one branch operation. The first one will be in L.A."

"So we'd move back out there?"

He nodded. "If you wouldn't mind."

"No." She smiled. "I wouldn't mind." Then she said, "Do you know what type of work they'd want to hire you for?"

"Actually, I'm hoping to run the whole branch," he said. "That's the position they need and if nothing else, being an army officer equipped me for organization." Then he grinned again. "The Long Gray Line is everywhere."

She stared at him. "What?"

"The Long Gray Line," he repeated. "The U.S. Military Academy grads are called that because of the uniforms we wore as cadets. Graduates of West Point have networking contacts all over the world.

A retired soldier who works for PSI graduated a few years ahead of me. One of Walker's buddies talked to a friend of mine who knew I might be job hunting and word got back to them."

"That's amazing. You didn't even go looking for this job, did you?"

"Not exactly. But I had already decided to take medical retirement so it might work out well. And I think I'd enjoy the challenge." He made a wry face. "I'd be bored to death doing the same old thing over and over every day."

"That's one reason I enjoy teaching," she said. "There's always something to challenge me. A child with a special need, a new approach to try, even parent meetings are rarely boring."

"I bet you're a good teacher," he said.

"I try to be. Teaching the next generation is one of the most important jobs there is, I believe." Then she gestured at the piles of paperwork in front of her. "And speaking of jobs, I'd better get back to work on these spelling tests."

"Ahh. Teacher talk." His smile flashed. "It turns me on."

Phoebe's hand paused, as she lifted her gaze to his. "Teacher talk turns you on?"

He rose from the easy chair and began to walk toward her. "Yeah. Wanna see?"

"Wade!" She made a token effort to scoot away as he grabbed her and pulled her against his body. "I've got to finish grading these papers. It won't take me long."

He paused. "How long?"

"Not long!" She twisted her arm so that she could see the face of her watch. "Ten minutes or so."

"Ten minutes? Sorry, can't wait that long."

"You're impossible," she said as he lowered his head and set his mouth on hers, then pulled her up against his body.

"Impossible to deter," he muttered against her skin, kissing his way along her jaw and sucking her earlobe into his mouth, swirling his tongue around it.

She felt her knees buckle beneath the sheer delight that being in his arms always brought. Wrapping her arms around his neck, she let her head fall back as her muscles went lax. Wade took immediate advantage of the exposed slender length of her neck, sliding his mouth down the warm, silken column, nuzzling aside the scooped top of the knit shirt to nip at her collarbone. Phoebe murmured with pleasure, her body humming, response blooming inside her.

He bent and slid his arms beneath her knees, sweeping her into his arms and carrying her up the stairs. She clutched at his neck as he took the steps two at a time. "I'm too heavy for this. You'll hurt yourself. Put me down."

He laughed aloud. "Do you know how many pounds I used to carry up the side of a mountain? Trust me, honey, you're not too heavy." He paused at the top for a deep kiss, sweeping his tongue into her mouth and enticing her into exploring him as well. "Besides," he said when he lifted his head, "when I was packing a load up a mountain, I didn't have this kind of incentive waiting for me at the top."

It took him only a moment to cover the steps to her bedroom, only a moment more to cross the room and set her beside the bed. Although she had steadfastly refused to allow herself to think of him during waking hours, she had dreamed of Wade over and over, even after she'd believed he was dead. But none of the dreams had ever come close to the heady reality of being in his arms. Even now, she wasn't sure it was real sometimes.

He pulled her shirt over her head as she set her small hands to work unbuttoning his, then unhooked her bra. She paused so that he could slide it off her shoulder and toss it aside, and then, as he cupped her breasts and began to lightly rub his thumbs across the rosy nipples, her hands slowed and fell away.

He tore his gaze from the sight of the plump,

beautiful mounds in his hands to look into her eyes. Heat and passion filled his gaze, and to her delight, she felt his body shudder in anticipation against her. Reluctantly, he took his hands from her and stripped off his jeans and briefs, then tugged her slacks and panties down and off in one smooth, efficient motion. He reached around her and peeled the bedcovers back before urging her down onto the cool cotton sheets.

Taking her hand, he guided it down between them to his aching length. "Help me."

He jumped when her small hand closed around him. Savoring the silken feeling of his body, so taut and hard, she tightened her grip the way she knew he liked and stroked him once, twice and yet again. His hips lifted and thrust against her and he growled. "Tease."

She lightly bit his shoulder. "Tell me you don't like it and I'll stop."

He sounded as if he were having trouble dragging air into his lungs. "Like that's ever going to—oh, baby, yeah."

As she positioned him at the throbbing entrance to her body, she lifted her hips. He was hot and solid and she cried out as he surged forward, embedding himself deeply within her. Her hands clenched on his buttocks, urging him to move, and within moments they established a fast, frantic rhythm that built a blazing fire within her. His body hammered against her, creating an ever-rising tension that stretched tighter and tighter until finally it snapped. As her body bucked and writhed in his arms, and then he was hoarsely calling her name as his body stiffened and froze in a shattering climax that left him shaking and gasping for breath.

When she could breathe again, think again, she stretched up and pressed a kiss to his shoulder. "Wow."

He snorted and chuckled. "Yeah. Wow." He rolled to one side and pulled her into his arms and she relaxed against him, enjoying the cuddling. "I think we've mastered that."

"You do? As an educator, I can tell you that research shows that even when a skill has been mastered, a certain amount of practice is necessary to reinforce the concept."

"Is that so?" He stroked a hand gently down over her hip and lightly squeezed her bottom. "In that case, I suppose we'll just have to keep practicing until we're sure we've got it right."

Now it was her turn to laugh. "Could take a while."

"It could," he agreed.

Nine

Wade had a job interview on Friday with the company out of Virginia, the specialized security firm that was setting up a new branch. He'd met the personnel director already, and today's interview, he told Phoebe, was with the owner of the company.

"He's going to love you." She picked up her coffee cup as he rose to put his dishes in the dishwasher. They'd gotten into a pleasant weekday routine in which they had breakfast together before she left. He usually had some kind of start on dinner before she arrived home, which meant she got her work done faster if she'd brought any home to grade, which meant that right after Bridget went to bed, she and Wade could go to bed, also.

Or at least go to the bedroom, she amended.

Every night he made love to her, stoking the blaze between them into a raging inferno of need. She awoke in his arms in the morning to a wild sense of unreality.

She'd had more than a year to accustom herself to the idea that Wade would not be a part of her life, and during half of that time she'd believed that he was dead. Sometimes it was difficult to believe that she really could be so happy. Although *happy* was a pale imitation of the feelings that rioted through her when she came through the door in the evening to see him there waiting for her, holding their daughter in the crook of one muscular arm.

When he pulled her to him and kissed her senseless, she was able to silence the one niggling voice in her head that reminded her that Wade might desire her…but he didn't love her.

"Don't worry about Bridget," she said. "Angie is watching her all day."

Wade nodded. "I could be back by lunch if this doesn't fly. If it does…it'll be late when I get home."

She rose on tiptoe to kiss him as he straightened his uniform, liking the way he'd said *home*. As if they truly were a family already. "Good luck."

She watched as he climbed into the rental car he still had, and waved as he drove off. "I love you," she murmured.

Would she ever be able to say it aloud? He seemed happy, and he clearly was thrilled with fatherhood. And when he touched her…well, they had no problems in that department. She smiled to herself as warmth radiated through her. But sometimes she caught him staring into space with a faraway expression on his face and she wondered what he was thinking about.

She was afraid she knew. And she was afraid to ask.

Melanie. Oh, she remembered everything that had happened the night of the reunion, the way he'd looked at her as if she were some new treasure he'd discovered—but that had been one single night. And even then, when he'd realized how upset Melanie had been, he'd been quick to pursue her.

To reassure her that there was nothing between Phoebe and him?

She would never know. Just as she would never know how much he still thought of her sister, how often his heart ached with loss.

Phoebe's insecurities, those feelings that had dominated her interactions with her sister most of her life, reared up and grabbed her attention every once in a while, reminding her that Wade had belonged to Melanie.

Never to her.

True, Wade seemed content now. But was it the familiarity of their friendship? His new fatherhood? Guilt at leaving her pregnant and alone? She feared it might be all three.

But he's with me now. He couldn't make love to me like that if he didn't care for me at least a little. Could he? Stop being a pessimist.

The school day dragged. She wondered how Wade's interview went. She checked her mobile phone for messages several times during the day, but he hadn't called. Although she hadn't expected him to, she worried that things hadn't gone well.

He probably wouldn't call her if the interview had not been successful. For all the years that she'd known him, Wade had been an intensely private man about his deepest feelings; she suspected that if he didn't want to talk, prying any information out of him would be next to impossible.

It wasn't until she saw the familiar outline of her little home that her spirits rose. Bridget was in there, with Angie. The sight of her daughter, the feel of that little body snuggled into her arms, was always balm to her sad moments.

Angie was sitting cross-legged on the couch, watching an afternoon soap opera, when Phoebe came through the door. "She was great today," Angie informed her. "I laid her down for her afternoon nap about two so she shouldn't get up again until at least four. I put the paper and the mail on the table."

"Thank you so much," Phoebe said. "I really appreciate you coming on short notice."

"Not a problem." Angie gathered her things. "Wish me luck on my psych test."

"Luck." Phoebe winked and smiled at her as Angie left. She set down her bag of paperwork from the day and slipped out of her shoes, then headed for the kitchen to get a drink.

As she sipped her tea, she glanced through the mail Angie had laid on the kitchen table. She set aside two bills and the grocery store flyer that had coupons in it, tossed three offers for credit cards in the trash, and laid out two envelopes of what looked like personal missives for immediate attention.

The first was a thank-you from a fellow teacher for whom she and her coworkers had thrown a bridal shower. The second bore an unfamiliar return address in California. Curious now, she slit the envelope and extracted a single sheet of paper.

Dear Mr. Merriman,

Mothers Against Drunk Driving (MADD) thanks you for your generous donation in memory of your loved one, Melanie Merriman. May we express our deepest condolences on your loss. Melanie sounds as if she was indeed a special young woman.

With your donation…

Bewildered, Phoebe picked up the envelope and looked more closely at the address. The sender had gotten Wade's name wrong on the envelope: it read Wade Merriman and she hadn't even noticed that it wasn't for her. Additionally, a change of address label had been slapped over the original and she realized it had been forwarded from his father's home in California.

She reread the letter—and suddenly it began to make sense, horrible sense, and the small, fragile bubble of hope she'd allowed herself to feel burst.

Wade had made a donation in Melanie's memory— *in his loved one's memory*—to a charitable organization known nationally for its education programs targeting drinking and driving. His *loved one*. Phoebe registered the hit to her heart as desolation spread through her and tears stung her eyes.

It wasn't that she begrudged the money, or the

thought. A part of her treasured the realization that her sister's name had been so honored. But now there was no way she could pretend that their marriage would be anything more than a convenience.

Now she knew for sure that there was no way Wade was ever going to love her because he was still in love with her sister. She sank down in a chair at the table and reread the letter twice more. Then she realized that if the letter hadn't been forwarded, she never would have known about the donation.

A sob escaped without warning. She clapped a hand over her mouth, but the truth confronting her wouldn't be denied and her efforts to resist the tears were futile. She had known Wade didn't love her. She shouldn't be so upset by this.

But she was. Not just upset, but devastated.

How could she marry him? Her heart wasn't going to be able to take that kind of beating day after day. She'd been kidding herself, believing that she could love him enough to make a marriage work. Even for the sake of her sweet baby girl sleeping upstairs, she couldn't do it.

At that thought, another sob welled up and tears began to stream down her face. Giving in to her misery, she laid her head down on her arms and cried.

Wade let himself into the house, wondering where Phoebe was. The baby monitor on the end table was silent, so she wasn't in Bridget's room. Could she be napping? Doubtful. He had yet to see her sleep during the day. Maybe she had taken Bridget out in the yard.

He crossed the living room and headed into the kitchen—and stopped short as he caught sight of her. She was slumped in a chair with her arms on the table, her head buried. Fear gripped him. "Phoebe! Sweetheart, what's the matter?" He rushed forward. Was she ill? Dear God, had something happened to Bridget? Panic nearly stopped his heart. "God, what's wrong? Is it Bridget?"

He knelt beside her chair and put an arm around her shoulders to hug her to him—and she exploded out of the chair halfway across the kitchen.

"Don't," she said between sobs. "Just—don't." She fumbled in a drawer for a tissue then turned away, her shoulders shaking with misery. "Bridget's fine."

A huge wave of relief swamped him momentarily, only to rush back as he realized she hadn't told him anything about herself. "Then what is it? Are you…" He could barely bear to utter the word. "Sick?"

She whipped back around at that, immediately grasping what he was asking. Her mother had gotten sick and died; so had his. "Oh, no, Wade. There's nothing wrong with me."

Except that there was. Her eyes were swollen from crying, her nose pink. She blotted her eyes and blew her nose while he stood. "Then…what?" he finally managed to ask.

She tried to smile, but her lips trembled and she quickly abandoned the effort. "I can't marry you."

What? "Why?" It was the most obvious question and he was too confused to think of a better one.

She sighed. "I just can't. It wouldn't be fair."

Fair to whom? "What the hell are you talking about?" Heat rose. He knew his tone was too rough, too angry, but— "Dammit, you scared me half to death! I thought something happened to Bridget or you. And now you tell me you won't marry me but you won't tell me why?"

A brittle silence followed the furious torrent of words, but she didn't speak, merely stood there with her eyes averted. And in her stance he read determination. He knew Phoebe and he knew that posture.

But what—? It hit him then. Stunned, he sank into the chair she'd bolted from. "It's because of Melanie, isn't it?"

She sucked in a sharp breath and nodded, and he saw a tear trickle down her cheek.

"Lord God above," he said quietly. Silence

reigned again as he absorbed the information. He'd wondered—no, he'd feared—for more than a year, that she blamed him for Melanie's death. It had kept him from contacting her after the first time they'd made love, and it had cost him the first months of his child's life.

When he'd finally decided to try to talk to her about it, she had been gone. And after he'd found her, after he'd learned about Bridget, his guilt had taken a backseat while he had adjusted to fatherhood and pretended that everything was fine and that Phoebe would love him and that they'd spend the rest of their lives together.

He scrubbed his hands over his face and looked down at the table, unable to stand seeing the pity and regret he knew he would see in her eyes.

A letter lay on the table and his name caught his eye. His first name, anyway. As he scanned it, he realized what it was. The foundation to which he'd made the donation in memory of Melanie had sent a thank-you note.

"I opened it by accident." Phoebe's tone was flat.

"I thought it would be a meaningful wedding gift."

"A *wedding gift?*"

"I'm sorry," he said. "I know there's nothing I can say to ever make it up to you—"

"You don't have to—"

"—and if it helps any, I will never forgive myself for letting Melanie die. If I'd been quicker, I'd have caught her. I've relived that night a thousand times and I know why you blame me." He halted for a moment. "I blame myself, so why shouldn't I expect you to?"

"Wade—"

"Don't." His shoulders slumped. "Just tell me what you want me to do now. Do you want me to leave?" His voice broke. "I will. I hope that you'll let me see Bridget sometimes, but I won't push—"

"Wade!"

At the volume and pitch of her voice, he finally stopped talking abruptly for the first time since she'd shoved away from his embrace.

Looking at the anguished set of his features, hearing the pain in his voice, she suddenly realized what he was thinking. It had nothing to do with lost love. *He was blaming himself for Melanie's death!* A tidal wave of shock, confusion and compassion crashed over her head and she forgot about her own pain.

"Wade," she said. He didn't look at her and she said it again, crossing to the table and touching his arm. "Wade, look at me."

Slowly, he lifted his gaze to hers and she was astounded by the pleading look in his eyes.

"I don't blame you," she whispered. She knelt on the floor beside his chair. "I've never blamed you. Melanie was impulsive. She had an ornery streak a mile wide. Her heart was that big, too, most of the time. She had been *drinking*. Neither one of us is responsible for what happened that night." She paused and put a hand to his face. "I don't blame you," she said again, urgently, as the look on his face eased fractionally.

"Then why?" He swallowed. "Why won't you marry me? God, Phoebe, I know I was a slow learner, but I realized that night at the dance that you were what had been missing from my life." He averted his eyes. "I took advantage of you after the funeral. I have no excuse, except that I had finally figured out that I loved you and I couldn't have walked away from you then any more than I could have stopped breathing."

He stopped speaking again then, and the only sound in the room was his harsh breathing and the hitching breaths she still took in the aftermath of her storm of tears.

Phoebe was frozen, his words hammering at her brain but not making sense. At least, not making sense in her current framework of reality.

"Phoebe?"

She sank down onto her heels and he looked alarmed. "I'm sorry. I shouldn't have—"

"You love me?"

He stopped. Searched her eyes, his own incredulous. "You didn't know?" He snorted. "I thought the whole damned world could see it."

"I didn't know," she confirmed. "I thought— believed that you still…"

"Melanie?"

She nodded. "When I saw the letter, I thought you'd done it because you still missed her, and that it was an accident that it came to this address."

"Oh, sweetheart, no." He put his hands beneath her elbows and stood, lifting her to her feet. "It was supposed to make you *happy*. I wanted to do something special to commemorate our marriage." He paused, looking down at her and she could see him choosing his words with care. "My feelings for your sister were only a crush. Infatuation. Mel and I weren't well suited. You surely could see that. We were over long before that reunion and I never regretted it."

As their eyes met again, she saw the beginnings of hope creeping into his expression. "You love me?" she said again. Stupid, she knew, but she wasn't quite sure she'd really heard it the first time.

His taut expression eased and the hope blossomed into a look that warmed her heart. "I love you," he said. "I've loved you since the night you asked me to dance and I realized I'd been chasing the wrong sister for a long time."

Her eyes filled with tears. "I love you, too," she said. "Oh, Wade, so much…" She smiled tremulously. "Pinch me. I must be dreaming."

"No way," he said. "Either the pinch or the dreaming. This is real, sweetheart. As real as that little girl sleeping upstairs." He gathered her against his body and pressed his forehead against hers. "Marry me, please, Phoebe?"

She tried to nod. "Yes. I would love to be your wife."

"Mother of my children," he prompted.

"Children? As in more than our one?" She slid her arms up around his neck and toyed with the collar of his shirt.

"Definitely more. Bridget would be spoiled stinking rotten if she was an only." He paused. "When did you realize…?"

"That I loved you?" She laughed. "At the risk of inflating your ego to an unforgivable level, I'll tell you. I can't remember when I didn't love you. I worshipped you when I was eight, nine, ten. I idolized you at eleven and twelve. By thirteen I was hopelessly infatuated. It tore me to pieces when you dated Mel."

"I never knew." His tone was wondering. "How could I not have known?"

"I wasn't exactly the most outgoing kid," she reminded him.

"Yeah, but you were always comfortable with me. You were—in love with me," he said ruefully. His expression changed. "God, I could really have blown it, couldn't I?"

She shrugged. "Doubt it."

Within ten minutes, he had her flat on her back in the big bed in her room. *Their* room, she amended silently. Soon she'd be giving herself and everything she had into his care.

Her attention abruptly veered back to the present as one warm, hairy leg pressed between her own legs and Wade's weight pressed her into the bed. She wriggled beneath him and he growled. "Wait."

"For what?" she teased, slipping her hands between them and rubbing his small, flat nipples into hard points.

"Tell me," he demanded, holding himself above her on his forearms, "that you felt it, too, that night we danced. Tell me it wasn't just me."

She slipped her hands down his back and he shuddered when he felt them moving lower, trying to pull him closer. Drawing back, he pushed slowly into the welcoming heat of her body, already soft and slick.

She murmured a sound of pleasure as she shifted her hips to accommodate him. "It wasn't just you." Then he lowered his head and claimed her mouth and she lost track of anything she'd intended to say as he began to move against her.

A short while later, she lay cuddled against his side. Wade was on his back, his arm around her idly caressing the ball of her shoulder, as another thought struck her. "Holy cow. I forgot all about your interview. How did it go?"

His hand stilled for a moment, then resumed its hypnotic rhythm. "Great!" She tilted her head back to see his face and he grinned at her. "I was offered the job."

"And you said yes." It was rhetorical and she was shocked when he shook his head in the negative.

"I said maybe," he said. His expression sobered, a sheepish quality creeping across his face. "I might have fibbed to you a little bit."

"Fibbed?" She was flabbergasted. "You made up the job?"

"No, no," he said hastily. "The job is real, and it's mine if I want it. But it's not in New York. In fact, it's not even on the East Coast."

"Where—? It's in California!" Could she get any more surprised? "Isn't it?"

"Southern California," he specified. "We'd have to move to San Diego if—"

"Yes!" She nearly shouted it in a totally un-Phoebe-like burst of enthusiasm as she pounded on his chest with her free hand. "You said yes, didn't you? We're going back?"

"I said it depended on my wife." He caught her and held her with ease as she flung herself atop him and wound her arms about his neck. "We wouldn't be in Carlsbad," he warned her. "I'd probably need to live somewhere closer to Mission Bay."

"Call them and tell them you'll take it!" She wriggled out of his arms and snatched up the portable telephone, thrusting the handset at him.

Wade laughed. "All right, all right. I'll do it in a few minutes." He paused, setting aside the phone and drawing her back into his arms. "Are you sure? I mean, I know you wanted to stay here and get tenure, and I can keep looking for a job around here if you'd rather not leave."

She detected the slightest trace of diffidence in his tone and her heart melted all over again. "You'd really do that for me?"

"For us," he qualified. "Wherever we decide to

live, I want you to be completely happy with the decision."

She sighed, sliding her hands into his hair and drawing his head down to hers. "Silly man. Don't you know I'd be happy anywhere with you?" She kissed him tenderly. "All I need is you, and our family. Going back to California would be wonderful, but all I really want is to spend the rest of my life with you."

And as he drew her back down to the bed, she realized the dream she'd had for so many years had truly become a reality. "I love you," she murmured.

"And I love you." He kissed her, then slid his hands down her body. "But I have to confess, that's not the *only* thing I want to do with you."

She laughed, too happy for words. Wade, the child they'd made together in love, and a future that looked as rosy as Bridget's cheeks. She thought of Melanie, and for the first time a true sense of peace filtered into Phoebe's heart. She had a hunch that wherever she was, Mel was doing a happy angel dance for her. And charming every male angel within sight.

* * * * *

SUMMER OF SECRETS

This exciting trilogy
continues in May with

STRICTLY LONERGAN'S BUSINESS

(SD #1724)

by *USA TODAY* bestselling author

MAUREEN CHILD

He'd never thought of his ever-efficient
assistant as a flesh-and-blood—desirable—
woman. Then the lights went out!

On Sale May 2006

And don't miss
SATISFYING LONERGAN'S HONOR,
available in June from Silhouette Desire.

Available at your favorite retail outlet!

If you enjoyed what you just read,
then we've got an offer you can't resist!

Take 2 bestselling love stories FREE!

Plus get a FREE surprise gift!

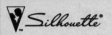

COMING NEXT MONTH

#1723 MR. AND MISTRESS—Heidi Betts
The Elliotts
Scandal threatens to rock the Elliott family when a business
mogul wants to make his pregnant mistress his wife!

#1724 STRICTLY LONERGAN'S BUSINESS—
Maureen Child
Summer of Secrets
She was his ever-dependent, quiet assistant...until a month of
sharing close quarters finally allowed her to catch her boss's eye.

#1725 THE RAGS-TO-RICHES-WIFE—Metsy Hingle
Secrets Lives of Society Wives
After a secret rendezvous leads to an unplanned pregnancy, this
Cinderella finds herself a high-society wife of convenience.

#1726 DEVLIN AND THE DEEP BLUE SEA—
Merline Lovelace
Code Name: Danger
He was a mystery to solve and she was just the woman to
uncover *all* of his secrets!

#1727 THE DURANGO AFFAIR—Brenda Jackson
Having an affair with a man like Durango was like lighting a
match during a drought—fast to ignite, hot to burn, impossible to
quench.

#1728 HOUSE OF MIDNIGHT FANTASIES—Kristi Gold
Rich and Reclusive
Reading your boss's mind can lead to trouble...*especially* when
you're the one he's fantasizing about.